McDougal Littell

Standardized Test Practice

Grade 7

McDougal Littell
A HOUGHTON MIFFLIN COMPANY
Evanston, Illinois • Boston • Dallas

Table of Contents

Grade 7 Science

INTRODUCTION

You can prepare for tests as you would for any other assignment you are given during the school year. The materials in this booklet will boost your achievement level in science.

CONTENT OVERVIEW

Each part of this booklet gives a different type of support that can become part of your daily study habits.

PART 1: GENERAL STRATEGIES FOR TAKING TESTS

Tips for Successful Testing This section gives strategies you can use during the school year to help you prepare for tests. It also provides tips you can use during the testing.

Vocabulary for Testing Situations In this section you'll find brief definitions of words often used on tests.

PART 2: TEST-TAKING STRATEGIES AND PRACTICE

This part of the book provides tutorials and practice in the types of items that appear on many types of science tests. You'll learn strategies for answering multiple-choice, constructed-response, and extended-response questions. Practice items usually include an *exhibit* followed by questions. Exhibits include the following:

- Reading passages
- Data tables
- Graphs
- Diagrams
- Maps

PART 3: TEST PRACTICE

This part of the book provides practice that will help you perform well on various types of questions commonly found on science tests. There are 66 practice questions that cover material that will increase your knowledge of science. After you have taken the practice test, check your answers to see how well you did. Notice the types of questions you missed and return to the strategies practice pages to improve your skill in answering questions.

General Strategies for Taking Tests

TIPS FOR SUCCESSFUL TESTING

There are many ways you can prepare for tests. These preparations can reinforce your daily learning in class, both in science and in other content areas. Knowledge of test-taking techniques doesn't replace knowledge of content, but it can help you learn how to use the test to demonstrate what you really know. You shouldn't lose points simply because you don't know how to take a test. The following tips give you some general suggestions on how to approach a test; you'll find more detailed instruction and practice in Part 2: Test-Taking Strategies and Practice.

DURING THE SCHOOL YEAR

1. **Master the content of your science courses.** The best way to prepare for tests is to study, understand, and review the content of your science class, whether you're taking life science, earth science, or physical science. Read your daily assignments carefully, and review the text and your classroom notes on a weekly basis. If you do these assignments, you will do well on tests.

2. **Practice with testing vocabulary.** Review the lists given in the next few pages. Your teacher may build some of these words into informal and formal assessments. For words that can be used in a variety of ways, make sure you understand the particular meaning the words have in the context of testing. Try to use science vocabulary during class and in homework assignments.

3. **Practice taking tests.** Use copies of past tests to practice taking a test with time limits. Learning how to use your time effectively is an important test-taking skill.

4. **Practice reading and interpreting visual representations of information.** Your textbook has many examples of data tables, diagrams, graphs, and maps. Become familiar with how these visuals work and the ways in which they present information.

5. **Interact with your own textbook.** Practice responding to assessment questions in your textbook, both orally and in writing. Try summarizing or paraphrasing longer passages.

6. **Build your ability to perform during long testing sessions.**
   a. Brainstorm appropriate ways to take short breaks during a timed session. You can try deep breathing, stretching, and so on.
   b. Think of strategies you've used before when you've had to concentrate for a long interval, and see how they might be applied to the testing situation.

7. **Learn to analyze the test questions.** Often, test questions seem awkward because they are written using language or formats that are unfamiliar or uncommon.
   a. Try paraphrasing the question in order to better understand it.
   b. Identify the type of information asked for in each question.

8. **Learn to skim materials.** Practice running your eyes quickly over texts, looking at headings, graphic features, and highlighted words. Learn to pick key words and phrases out of materials.

9. **Discuss test experiences immediately afterward.** After classroom tests and quizzes throughout the year, talk with your teacher and classmates about the experience. What strategies did you and your classmates use to come up with answers? How successful were these strategies?

SEVERAL WEEKS BEFORE THE TEST

As the date for a test approaches, begin to prepare for the types of items you might find in the test. Here are some general tips you'll have a chance to practice later in this book.

1. **Multiple-Choice Questions** In a well-constructed item, each wrong answer represents a mistake that might be made by a test taker who is careless or doesn't know the material. Use the following strategies with multiple-choice items.

   a. Read and consider the question (this part is called the *stem*) carefully *before* reading the alternative answer choices. Try to answer the question without using the choices.

   b. Pay close attention to key words in the question. For instance, look for the word NOT, as in "Which of the following is NOT an igneous rock?"

   c. Consider all the alternatives before making a choice.

   d. Eliminate any answers that you know are wrong. Often you will be able to eliminate choices that are weaker than the others, leaving a choice between the strongest two.

   - Look for two choices that describe the same idea. Both must be wrong.
   - Read the stem and each answer as a sentence. Does this sentence make grammatical and logical sense? Eliminate choices that do not "read in" logically.
   - When an answer includes an absolute word, it may be incorrect. Look for words like *always, never, none, all,* and *only* as a hint.

   e. When in doubt about an answer, try these ideas to find the correct answer:

   - If one choice is much longer and more detailed than the others, it is often the correct answer.
   - If a word in a choice also appears in the stem, it should be strongly considered as the correct choice.
   - If two choices are direct opposites, one of them likely is the correct answer.
   - If one choice includes one or more of the other choices, it is often the correct answer.
   - If *some* or *often* is used in a choice, it should be strongly considered as the correct answer.
   - If *all of the above* is a choice, determine whether at least two of the other choices seem appropriate before selecting it.
   - If one response is more precise, it is more likely to be correct than a general response.

2. **Constructed-Response Items** Constructed-response items can have many forms. You may have to read a paragraph, graph, chart, map, or graphic organizer to extract information and to make an inference or draw a conclusion. You might have to create a map, graph, or graphic organizer yourself. Use these strategies for approaching a constructed-response item.

   a. Read the directions, also called the *prompt*, and analyze the steps required. Read through the entire prompt before answering.

   b. Look for key words in the prompt and plan your answer accordingly. Does the question ask you to identify a cause-and-effect relationship or to compare and contrast? Are you looking for a sequence or making a generalization?

c. Plan your answer. If you are writing more than a few words, jot down notes and supporting details you may wish to use in your response.

d. Target your answer. When writing your response, don't just include everything you can think of, hoping that some part of it will be correct.

e. Support your statements with examples and details.

3. **Extended-Response Items** Extended-response questions, like constructed-response questions, include a prompt and usually focus on an exhibit of some kind. However, they are more complex and require more time to complete than short-answer constructed-response questions. Use the following strategies with extended-response items.

a. Carefully read the prompt and determine what it asks you to do.

b. Analyze the exhibit and make notes on material that may apply to the question.

c. If the question requires an essay or other piece of writing, write ideas in outline form. Use the outline to write your answer.

DURING THE TEST

Keep the following points in mind while taking a test.

1. **Read the directions carefully.** There may be slight differences among similar directions that could make a significant difference in how you approach the test.

2. **Take a second look.** Recheck your answers to make sure you haven't made a mistake in your markings.

3. **Pay special attention when using a separate answer sheet.** It is easy to drop down one line and accidentally throw off the answers. Use any or all of the following techniques.

a. Use a guide, such as a ruler, on the answer sheet to keep from marking answers on the wrong line.

b. Check every five answers or so to make sure that the appropriate line is filled for each answer.

c. Each time you turn a page, make sure the question and answer lines match.

d. Fill in blanks carefully and neatly and do not make stray pencil marks.

e. Fold the test booklet so that only one page is showing at a time.

4. **If you don't know the answer, make an educated guess.** When there is no penalty for guessing on a multiple-choice item, it's better to guess at an answer than to leave it blank. Try to eliminate one or two choices first.

5. **Rely on facts or data in the question—not on personal preferences— when answering questions.** Pay close attention to information provided in graphs, charts, or diagrams when coming up with your answer.

6. **Plan your time.** Answering all of the questions will increase your chances for a better score, so you should make sure to finish the test. Pay attention to the time, and work to maintain an appropriate pace. Calculate in advance how many questions you need to answer by the halfway mark, but remember that some question formats may take you longer than others.

Vocabulary for Testing Situations

The following vocabulary words can help you prepare for tests. The vocabulary list contains words often used in test materials. The definitions show how each word would most likely be used in a test situation but may not be the only definitions.

TEST VOCABULARY

according to *(preposition)* as stated in

affect *(verb)* influence, change

analyze *(verb)* break down into parts and explain relationships among the parts

apparent *(adjective)* clear, obvious

appropriate *(adjective)* suitable, correct

argument *(noun)* reason offered in proof for or against an idea

characterize *(verb)* represent, symbolize, show qualities of

classified *(adjective)* arranged into groups according to similarities

combined *(adjective)* joined, united

compare/contrast *(verb)* describe similarities and differences

condition *(noun)* situation, circumstances

contribute *(verb)* add to, assist

correspond to *(verb)* match, fit

current *(adjective)* at the present time

data *(noun)* information collected by observing or experimenting

define *(verb)* give the exact meaning of

depend upon *(verb)* be controlled by something else

describe *(verb)* give important information about

determine *(verb)* decide

development *(noun)* progress, growth

draw a conclusion *(verb)* make a judgment based on certain ideas

emphasize *(verb)* stress, focus on, feature

evaluate *(verb)* judge the value of

event *(noun)* something that happens in a particular time/place

example *(noun)* illustration, representation

except *(conjunction)* all but, everything other than

excerpt *(noun)* selection, portion of a text

expanding *(adjective)* growing, increasing

explain *(verb)* make clear and understandable

former *(adjective)* previous, earlier

foundation *(noun)* base, support for conclusion

generalization *(noun)* general statement based on many examples

graph *(noun)* visual representation of facts/figures

identify *(verb)* find, pick out

impact *(verb)* affect, influence

indicate *(verb)* show, point out

inference *(noun)* a conclusion based on deduction, an informed guess

intent *(noun)* plan, design

interpret *(verb)* give your opinion, supported with reasons and details

involve *(verb)* include as part of

major *(adjective)* important, significant

minor *(adjective)* small, insignificant

occur *(verb)* happen

passage *(noun)* part of a written work

point *(noun)* position, main idea

primary *(adjective)* main, most important

principle *(noun)* a basic law or truth

probably *(adverb)* most likely

provide *(verb)* offer, supply

refer *(verb)* to use a source of information

regulate *(verb)* control, manage

relate *(verb)* show the relationship or link between things

result *(noun)* finding; effect

select *(verb)* choose

sequence *(verb)* to arrange in order

significant *(adjective)* important, meaningful

similar *(adjective)* nearly alike

topic *(noun)* subject

valid *(adjective)* logical

2 | Test-Taking Strategies and Practice

MULTIPLE CHOICE

A multiple-choice question consists of a stem and a set of choices. One of the choices correctly answers the question or completes the sentence.

❶ Read the stem carefully and try to answer the question or complete the sentence without looking at the choices.

❷ Pay close attention to key words in the stem. They may direct you toward the correct answer.

❸ Read each choice with the stem. Don't jump to conclusions about the correct answer until you've read all of the choices.

❹ Think carefully about questions that include *all of the above* among the choices.

❺ After reading all of the choices, eliminate any that you know are incorrect.

❻ Use modifiers to help narrow your choice.

❼ Look for the best answer among the remaining choices.

Improve your test-taking skills by practicing the strategies discussed in this section. Read the tips on the strategies page. Then apply them to the practice items on the next two pages. Use the Thinking Through the Answers that follows the practice pages to help you evaluate your answers to the practice items.

SCIENCE SAMPLE

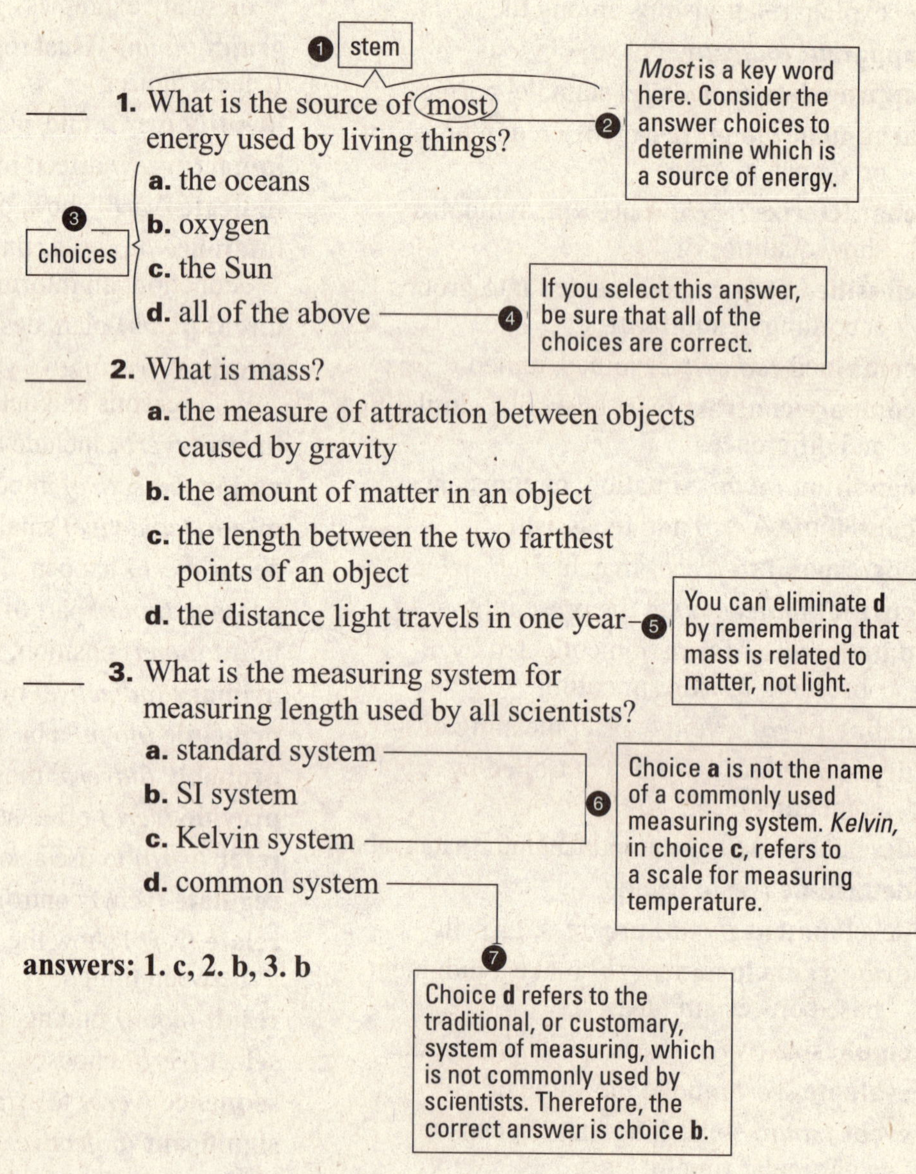

Practice

SCIENCE SAMPLE

Directions: Read each question carefully and choose the BEST answer from the four choices.

_____ 1. Which activity is done by all living things?
  a. seeing
  b. hearing
  c. growing
  d. thinking

_____ 2. Which is a physical characteristic of minerals?
  a. hardness
  b. luster
  c. streak
  d. all of the above

_____ 3. What type of rock always forms when magma cools and hardens?
  a. sedimentary
  b. metamorphic
  c. igneous
  d. fossil

_____ 4. What are three common states of matter?
  a. chemical, physical, neutral
  b. solid, liquid, gas
  c. rough, smooth, clear
  d. cold, warm, hot

Practice

SCIENCE SAMPLE

Directions: Read each question carefully and choose the BEST answer from the four choices.

_____ **1.** Which process describes digestion?
   a. taking in oxygen and releasing carbon dioxide
   b. ridding the body of waste products
   c. producing offspring
   d. breaking down food into simpler substances

_____ **2.** Which is a definition of a stimulus?
   a. where an organism lives
   b. the daily activities of an organism
   c. a signal that an organism responds to
   d. all of the above

_____ **3.** What happens when two objects having like charges are brought close together?
   a. They repel each other.
   b. They are attracted to each other.
   c. They neither repel nor attract.
   d. First they attract, and then they repel.

_____ **4.** Which is a heterogeneous mixture?
   a. a stick of butter
   b. a tossed salad
   c. a cup of hot tea
   d. all of the above

Answers

THINKING THROUGH THE ANSWERS

Questions from Page 11:

1. **c** is correct. All living things grow.

   a, b, and **d** are incorrect. Plants are living things, but they do not see, hear, or think.

2. **d** is correct. Hardness, luster, and streak are all physical characteristics of minerals, so *all of the above* is the BEST answer.

   a, b, and **c** by themselves alone are incorrect. All of these are physical characteristics of minerals. When more than one choice is correct, look for an answer choice such as *all of the above.*

3. **c** is correct. Igneous rocks are formed by the cooling and hardening of hot liquid rock.

   a is incorrect. Sedimentary rocks are formed from sediments that have been pressed and cemented together.

   b is incorrect. Metamorphic rocks are formed when sedimentary and igneous are changed by heat, pressure, and chemical reaction.

   d is incorrect. A fossil is evidence of the remains of a once-living thing.

4. **b** is correct. Solid, liquid, and gas are the three common states of matter.

   a, c, and **d** are incorrect. None of these are states of matter.

Questions from Page 12:

1. **d** is correct. In digestion, the body breaks down food into simpler substances that it can use.

   a is incorrect. Taking in oxygen and releasing carbon dioxide is respiration.

   b is incorrect. Ridding the body of waste products is excretion.

   c is incorrect. The production of offspring is reproduction.

2. **c** is correct. Stimuli are signals to which an organism responds.

   a and **b** are incorrect. These are not stimuli.

   d is incorrect. Do not choose an inclusive answer such as *all of the above* unless you are certain that more than one of the other choices are correct.

3. **a** is correct. Like charges always repel one another.

   b, c, and **d** are incorrect. Like charges only repel, so choice **a** is the only correct answer.

4. **b** is correct. A tossed salad is a mixture that is heterogeneous, or not the same throughout.

   a and **c** are incorrect. A stick of butter and hot tea are homogeneous mixtures that are the same throughout.

   d is incorrect. Only one choice gives a correct answer.

Strategies

CONSTRUCTED RESPONSE

Constructed-response questions focus on an exhibit, such as a passage, diagram, table, graph, or timeline. Instead of picking one answer from a set of choices, you write a short response. Sometimes, you can find the answer in the exhibit. Other times, you will use what you already know about a subject to answer the question.

❶ Read the title of the exhibit to get an idea of what it is about.

❷ Study the exhibit.

❸ Read the questions carefully. Study the exhibit again to find the answers.

❹ Write your answers. You don't need to use complete sentences unless the directions say so.

SCIENCE SAMPLE

Plant and Animal Cells ❶

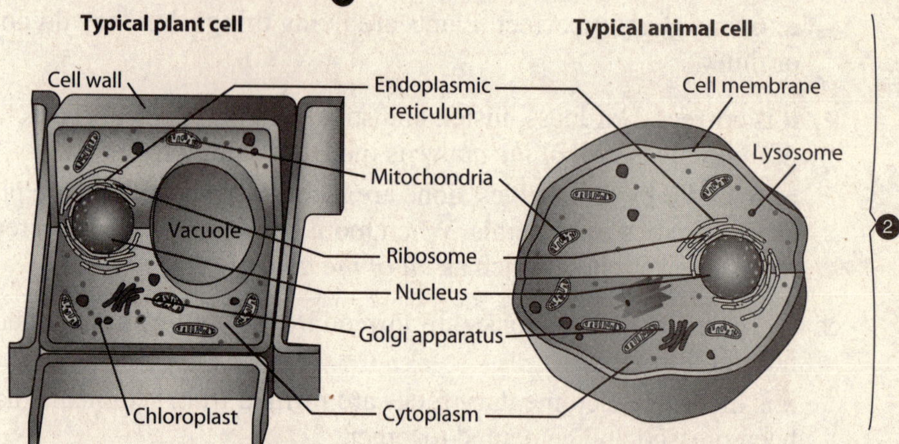

1. Compare the structures and features of plant and animal cells. Use at least ten terms to complete the diagram below to explain similarities and differences.

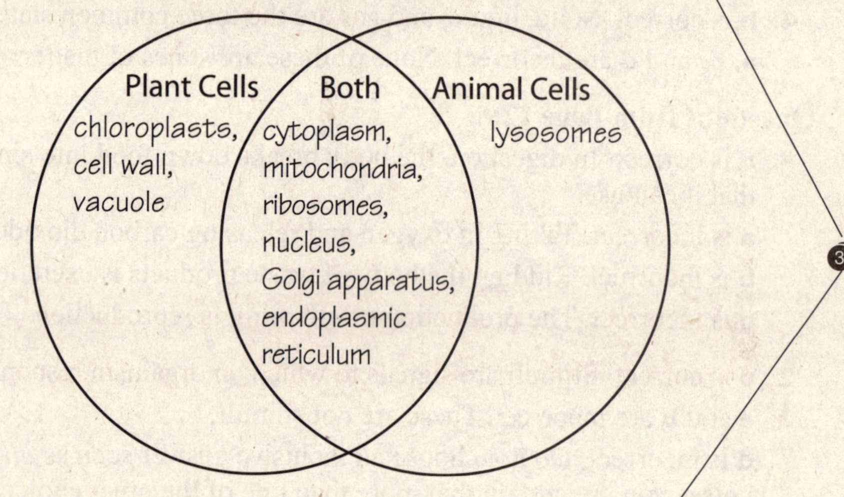

2. What function performed by plant cells involves chloroplasts?

❹ Chloroplasts capture light energy from the sun. They are the centers of photosynthesis, the process plants use to transform light, carbon dioxide, and water into usable energy and materials.

Practice

SCIENCE SAMPLE

Directions: Read the paragraph. Use the information you read and what you know about life science and animal habitats to answer the questions.

Camouflage

Many animals have marking or colorings that help them hide from other animals. Some animals have markings such as stripes and spots, allowing them to blend into a grassy or leafy environment. The covering of some animals changes colors with the season or, as with the chameleon, with any change in the environment. Camouflage sometimes protects animals from predators. Other times, it helps predators stay hidden long enough to catch their prey. In either case, camouflage is an important adaptation that aids the survival of many animals.

1. A spring cankerworm is a caterpillar that feeds on leaves of trees. It has a brownish color. Why might predators have a hard time seeing spring cankerworms?

   ____

   ____

2. Polar bears are large and white. They live on the shores of the Arctic Ocean. They are hunters that feed mostly on seals, sea birds, and fish. How does the polar bear's coloring help it as a hunter?

   ____

   ____

3. Albinism is a condition in which an animal does not have any color in its skin, hair, or eyes. Suggest why albino animals, such as an albino mouse or alligator, rarely live to adulthood.

   ____

   ____

Practice

SCIENCE SAMPLE

Directions: Use the circle graph and the information provided to answer the
following questions. Use complete sentences for your answers.

Land Use

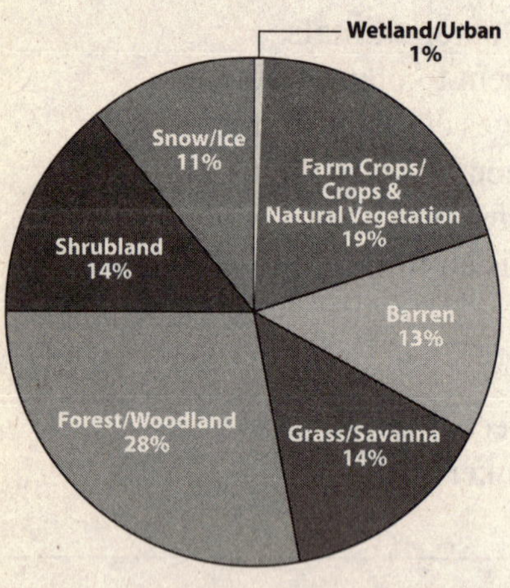

Source: *The Times Atlas of the World*

Only about 19 percent of land in the world is usable for food production. As the world
population increases, demand for food products—and for land on which to produce
it—goes up. For thousands of years, humans have been striving to transform areas into
farmable land. Innovations such as improved irrigation systems and terracing have
opened the possibility for sustainable farming in areas once thought unusable.

1. What percentage of land is used currently for farming?

2. Make a bar graph showing the information about *Land Use*.

3. Compare the bar graph and the circle graph. Which is better for showing parts of a whole?

Answers

THINKING THROUGH THE ANSWERS

Questions from Page 15:

1. A spring cankerworm has the coloring of tree trunks and branches. This camouflage helps hide it from predators.

2. The white polar bear blends in with the color of the ice and snow of the arctic environment. This camouflage makes it more difficult for its prey to see the polar bear.

3. Because albino animals have no skin or hair color, they appear white and cannot blend in with their environments. An albino mouse would be very easy for a predator to see and catch. Because an albino alligator would also be very easy to see, it would be difficult for the alligator to sneak up on its prey.

Questions from Page 16:

1. The graph shows that 19% is currently usable for farming.

2.

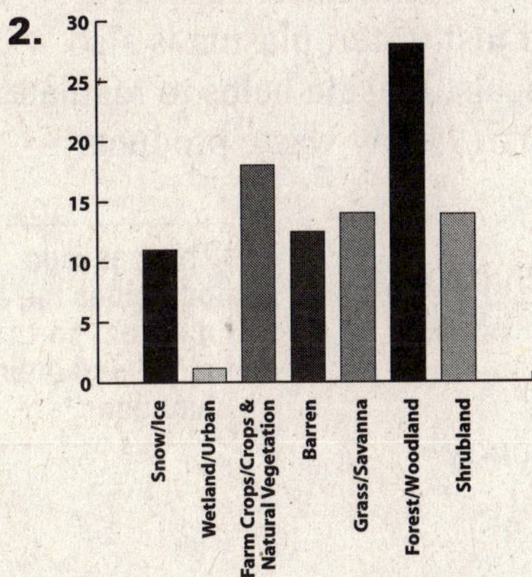

3. Possible answer: The circle graph is easier to use to identify parts of a whole. Both graphs make it easy to compare ways the land is used.

Strategies

READING PASSAGE

Sometimes you will need to read a passage to answer a question. Science textbooks contain factual information that is not always accompanied by a diagram or other visual representation. Read scientific writing carefully, and use context clues to unlock the meaning of unfamiliar words. Often, more than one question is associated with the same reading passage.

❶ Read the title.

❷ Skim the passage to get an idea of what it is about.

❸ Look for main ideas. After reading, ask, "What was this passage about?"

❹ Examine the sequence of ideas. They may be presented in the order in which they occur, which is called chronological order, or organized in some other way.

❺ Ask yourself questions about the passage as you read.

❻ Review the questions. This will give your reading a purpose and also help you find the answers more easily. Then read the passage.

SCIENCE SAMPLE

Blood ❶

Blood is more than just a red liquid moving through the body by blood vessels. When blood is seen through a microscope, several different solid parts are visible. Blood performs its health-giving jobs by circulating constantly—an ability that most other cells do not have.

Red blood cells give blood its red color. These doughnut-shaped disks carry oxygen to all the cells in the body, and they carry away carbon dioxide from the cells. White blood cells form part of the immune system. ❷ ❸ They defend the body against infection and disease by wrapping around an invading germ and destroying it. Platelets are blood cells that help the blood clot when a person gets a cut. ❹

Blood also has a liquid part called plasma. Plasma makes up about 55 percent of the blood. This liquid is not just water; plasma is also made up of protein, salt, and other chemicals. Plasma helps to regulate the body's internal temperature, and it carries away waste products from the cells.

> This passage describes the different parts of blood and their functions.

_____ 1. According to the passage, which of these functions is NOT performed by blood?

    a. bringing oxygen to cells

    b. distributing heat around the body

    c. stimulating physical growth

    d. forming clots

_____ 2. What is the largest component of blood?

    a. plasma

    b. red blood cells

    c. white blood cells

    d. platelets

_____ 3. In what way are blood cells different from other cells in the body?

    a. Most cells in the body are made up of protein, but blood cells are not.

    b. Blood cells are liquid, but most other cells are solid.

    c. Most cells in the body can fight infections, but blood cells cannot.

    d. Blood cells are always moving, while most other cells stay in one place.

answers: 1. c, 2. a, 3. d

Practice

SCIENCE SAMPLE

Directions: The passage is about the potential use of fusion as an energy source. Use this passage and your knowledge of science to answer the questions.

The Sun's Fuel

Fusion is the process by which energy is produced in the Sun and other stars. During fusion, two isotopes of hydrogen—deuterium and tritium—combine, or fuse, to form helium. During fusion, an enormous amount of energy is released. This process is spontaneous and occurs constantly in the Sun. However, on Earth fusion is dangerous and can cause explosions such as that of a hydrogen bomb. Some scientists think fusion is the answer to the world's energy needs. The oceans contain plenty of deuterium. A liter of ocean water equals the energy potential of 300 liters of gasoline. However, critics argue that the amount of energy needed to cause the reaction is very high and fusion will be too costly and dangerous.

_____ **1.** The two isotopes involved in fusion on the Sun are deuterium and
- **a.** helium.
- **b.** water.
- **c.** gasoline.
- **d.** tritium.

_____ **2.** Why are critics of fusion as an energy resource skeptical about its usefulness?
- **a.** Fusion is too dangerous and too expensive.
- **b.** Energy from fusion would be so cheap it would damage the world's economy.
- **c.** Fossil fuels will supply all the energy people will ever need.
- **d.** Fusion would reduce the Sun's ability to produce energy.

_____ **3.** Which contains a source of deuterium?
- **a.** the ocean
- **b.** the Sun
- **c.** hydrogen bombs
- **d.** gasoline

Practice

SCIENCE SAMPLE

Directions: The passage explains some arguments about the use of space flights with human crews. Use this passage and your knowledge of science to answer the questions.

The Future of Astronauts

Before astronauts orbited Earth and landed on the moon, space probes had been traveling through our solar system and collecting information. Many consider astronauts to be unnecessary for space exploration. Especially in the wake of space shuttle tragedies, critics argue that space missions with crews are much too dangerous. There are many advantages to robot spacecraft. Robots do not need food, sleep, and other materials and conditions that humans need. Robots can travel much farther for longer periods of time and do not have to be returned when a mission is completed. However, others argue that humans are an important part of space exploration because they can react more quickly to unusual or unexpected events.

_____ **1.** Why do critics of space exploration by human crews think astronauts should be grounded?

    a. They are not necessary.

    b. The job is too dangerous.

    c. Robot spacecraft are better suited for exploration.

    d. all of the above

_____ **2.** Why do others consider astronauts to be an important component of space exploration?

    a. They are easier to replace than robot spacecraft.

    b. They can deal with unusual and unexpected events better.

    c. They weigh much less than most robot spacecraft.

    d. They can travel much farther than robot spacecraft.

_____ **3.** What are some other reasons for continuing space missions with human crews?

    a. a human's ability to reason and solve problems

    b. to study the effects of space environments on humans

    c. to fulfill the human desire for exploration

    d. all of the above

Answers

THINKING THROUGH THE ANSWERS

Questions from Page 19:

1. **d** is correct. Deuterium and tritium fuse to form helium.

   a is incorrect. Helium is the product of solar fusion.

   b and **c** are incorrect. Neither water nor gasoline is an isotope.

2. **a** is correct. Critics argue that the radiation produced by fusion will be too costly and dangerous to clean up.

   b is incorrect. This statement is not supported by the text.

   c and **d** are incorrect. These choices present inaccurate ideas.

3. **a** is correct. The passage indicates that the ocean contains a lot of deuterium, making it a cheap and easy source.

   b is incorrect. While fusion occurs in the Sun, it is not a source for fusion energy on Earth.

   c is incorrect. The energy from hydrogen bombs cannot be harnessed safely.

   d is incorrect. Gasoline does not produce fusion power.

Questions from Page 20:

1. **d** is correct. Critics of space exploration by human crews consider robot spacecraft to be better suited for space exploration. They think astronauts are not necessary and that the job is too dangerous.

   a, b, and **c** are incorrect. All of these are reasons that critics think space exploration should not be done by human crews. When more than one choice is correct, look for an inclusive answer choice such as *all of the above.*

2. **b** is correct. Usually humans can react more quickly to unusual or unexpected events.

   a is incorrect. It is clearly an untrue statement.

   c is incorrect. It is not supported by the text.

   d is incorrect. It is contradicted by the text.

3. **d** is correct. Humans have superior abilities of reasoning and problem solving. Also, space exploration with human crews offers the opportunity to study the effects of space environments on humans, as well as to satisfy people's interest in exploration.

   a, b, and **c** are incorrect. All of these are reasons that support continued space missions with human crews. When more than one choice is correct, look for a choice such as *all of the above.*

Strategies

DATA TABLES

Charts present information in a visual form. Science textbooks use several types of charts, including tables, flow charts, Venn diagrams, and concept webs. The type of chart most commonly found in standardized tests is the table. It organizes information in columns and rows for easy viewing.

❶ Read the title and identify the broad subject of the table.

❷ Read the headings of columns and rows in addition to any labels. This will provide more details about the subject of the table.

❸ Compare and contrast the information from column to column and row to row.

❹ Try to draw conclusions from the information in the table. Ask yourself: *What patterns does the table show?*

❺ Read the questions, and then study the table again.

SCIENCE SAMPLE

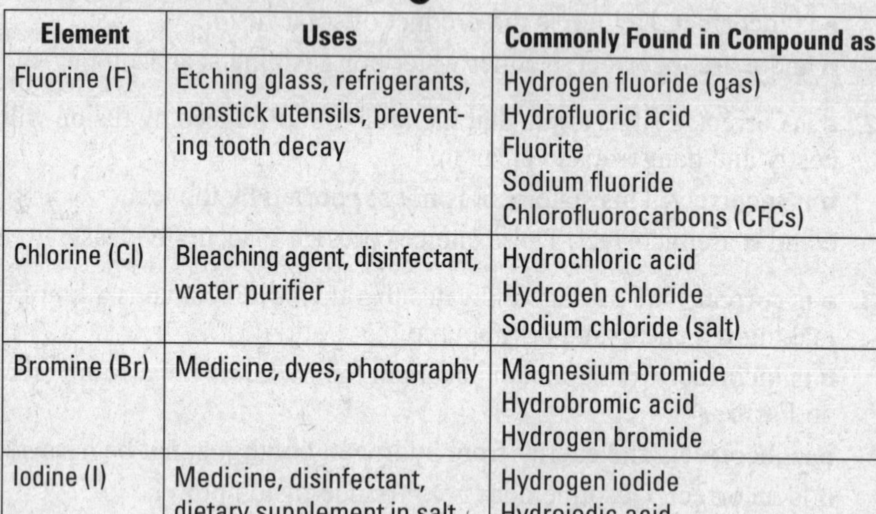

Uses of Some Elements ——❶

❷ Element	Uses	Commonly Found in Compound as
Fluorine (F)	Etching glass, refrigerants, nonstick utensils, preventing tooth decay	Hydrogen fluoride (gas) Hydrofluoric acid Fluorite Sodium fluoride Chlorofluorocarbons (CFCs)
Chlorine (Cl)	Bleaching agent, disinfectant, water purifier	Hydrochloric acid Hydrogen chloride Sodium chloride (salt)
Bromine (Br)	Medicine, dyes, photography	Magnesium bromide Hydrobromic acid Hydrogen bromide
Iodine (I)	Medicine, disinfectant, dietary supplement in salt	Hydrogen iodide Hydroiodic acid Silver iodide

_____ **1.** Consider the uses listed. What generalization can you make about the elements shown in the table?

a. These elements have uses related to water purification.

b. These elements are all disinfectants.

c. These elements do not easily form compounds.

d. These elements have many uses related to health and medicine.

_____ **2.** Which element is added to salt as a dietary supplement?

a. fluorine

b. chlorine

c. bromine

d. iodine

_____ **3.** One similarity between chlorine and iodine is that they are both used

a. in medicines.

b. as bleaching agents.

c. as disinfectants.

d. in dyes.

answers: 1. d, 2. d, 3. c

Practice

SCIENCE SAMPLE

Directions: Use the exhibit to answer the questions.

Periodic Table of Some Elements

Source: http://pearl1.lanl.gov/periodic/default.htm

_____ **1.** What is the atomic number of aluminum?

    a. 5

    b. 13

    c. 26.98

    d. 31

_____ **2.** What is the atomic mass of bromine?

    a. 79.90

    b. 35

    c. 10.81

    d. 83.80

_____ **3.** What is the symbol for arsenic?

    a. Ar

    b. As

    c. Se

    d. Ac

Practice

SCIENCE SAMPLE

Directions: Use the table showing the Mohs hardness scale to answer the questions.

Mohs Hardness Scale

Mineral	Hardness	Common Tests
Talc	1	Scratched by fingernail
Gypsum	2	
Calcite	3	Scratched by penny
Fluorite	4	Scratched by a knife blade or window glass
Apatite	5	
Feldspar	6	Scratches a knife blade or window glass
Quartz	7	
Topaz	8	
Corundum	9	
Diamond	10	Scratches all common materials

_____ **1.** A copper penny has a hardness of 3.5, according to the scale. What could the penny scratch besides talc?

    a. feldspar and apatite

    b. fluorite and quartz

    c. topaz and diamond

    d. gypsum and calcite

_____ **2.** What is the hardness of glass if it can scratch apatite and be scratched by feldspar?

    a. less than 5

    b. between 5 and 6

    c. between 6 and 7

    d. greater than 7

_____ **3.** Since diamond is the hardest mineral on the scale, which is the only mineral listed that can scratch a diamond?

    a. corundum

    b. quartz

    c. another diamond

    d. feldspar

Answers

THINKING THROUGH THE ANSWERS

Questions from Page 23:

1. **b** is correct. The atomic number, or number of protons in the nucleus, of an atom of aluminum is 13.

   a and **d** are incorrect. Make sure you are reading the correct row and column in a table. 5 is the atomic number for boron, which is above aluminum in the table, and 31 is the atomic number for gallium, which is below aluminum.

   c is incorrect. The atomic mass of aluminum is 26.98.

2. **a** is correct. The atomic mass of bromine is 79.90.

   b is incorrect. The atomic number of bromine is 35.

   c is incorrect. Read the question carefully to avoid careless errors. 10.81 is the atomic mass of boron, not bromine.

   d is incorrect. Make sure you are reading the correct row and column in a table. 83.80 is the atomic mass for krypton, which is to the right of bromine in the table.

3. **b** is correct. As is the symbol for arsenic.

   a, c, and **d** are incorrect. Read the table carefully rather than jumping to conclusions. Ar is argon, Se is selenium, and Ac is actinium, an element not shown in this portion of the periodic table.

Questions from Page 24:

1. **d** is correct. Gypsum and calcite are softer than a copper penny, according to the table.

   a, b, and **c** are incorrect. Feldspar, apatite, fluorite, quartz, topaz, and diamond are all harder than copper.

2. **b** is correct. On the Mohs hardness scale, apatite is 5 and feldspar is 6. So if glass can scratch apatite and be scratched by feldspar, then its hardness must be between 5 and 6.

   a, c, and **d** are incorrect. Read the scale and the question carefully. The information in the chart helps eliminate these choices.

3. **c** is correct. Only a diamond could scratch another diamond.

   a, b, and **d** are incorrect. Corundum, quartz, and feldspar are all softer than diamond.

Strategies

GRAPHS

Graphs show data in a visual form. Line graphs are particularly useful for showing changes over time. Bar graphs make it easy to compare numbers or sets of numbers. Circle graphs show comparisons of parts to a whole.

❶ Read the title and identify the broad subject of the graph.

❷ Study labels; on vertical and horizontal axes, see the types of information presented in the graph. Note the intervals between amounts and time. These strategies will help you read graphs more efficiently.

❸ Look at the source line and evaluate the reliability of the information in the graph.

❹ Study the information in the graph and note any patterns.

❺ Draw conclusions and make generalizations based on these patterns.

❻ Read the questions carefully, and then study the graph again.

SCIENCE SAMPLE

Gases in Earth's Atmosphere ❶

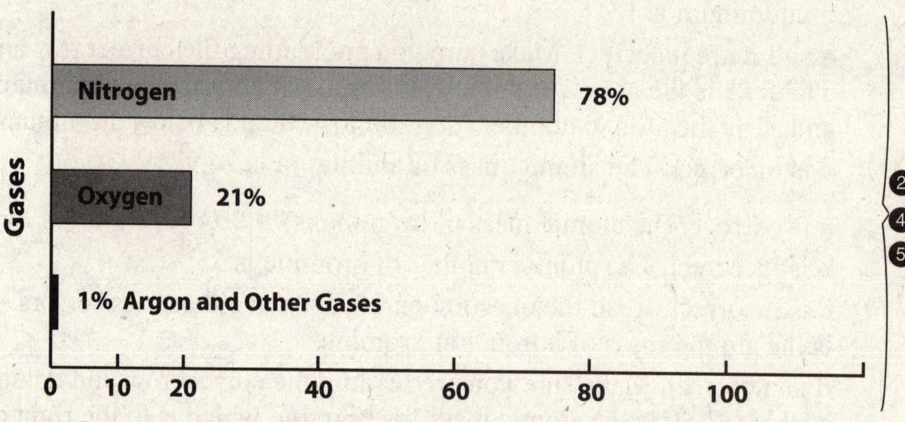

Source: *The World Book Encyclopedia,* 2003

_____ **1.** How much of Earth's atmosphere is composed of nitrogen and oxygen?

   a. 21%

   b. 78%

   c. 99%

   d. less than 1%

_____ **2.** The majority of the atmosphere is made up of

   a. oxygen.

   b. carbon dioxide.

   c. nitrogen.

   d. other gases.

_____ **3.** How much of Earth's atmosphere is composed of argon?

   a. 21%

   b. 78%

   c. 99%

   d. less than 1% ———— ❻

> Argon, together with other gases, makes up only 1 percent of Earth's atmosphere. Argon alone, therefore, makes up less than 1 percent. The correct answer is choice **d.**

answers: 1. c, 2. c, 3. d

Practice

SCIENCE SAMPLE

Directions: Use the line graph and information provided to answer the questions.

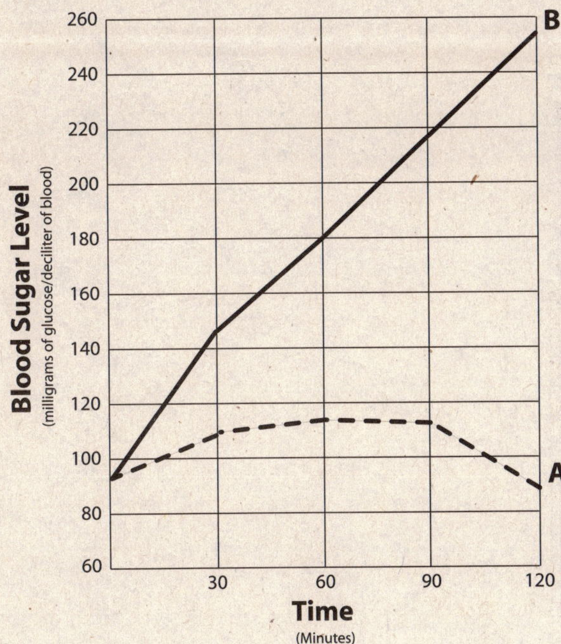

Source: http://www.brist.plus.com

This graph shows the blood sugar levels of two people in the two hours immediately following a typical meal.

_____ **1.** Insulin helps the body remove sugar from the blood, but people with diabetes produce little or no insulin. Which line on this graph could represent the blood sugar of a person with diabetes?

    a. line A, because it shows a lower level of insulin

    b. line B, because it shows a greater drop in the insulin level

    c. line A, because it shows a lower level of sugar in the blood

    d. line B, because it shows a higher level of sugar in the blood

_____ **2.** If the person with diabetes was given insulin, how would the graph change?

    a. Line A would have a higher spike as a result of the increase in insulin.

    b. The two lines would be closer, indicating that sugar was being removed from the blood at a similar rate.

    c. Line B would go down first and then up.

    d. Line B would become straight, indicating that the blood sugar levels remained constant.

_____ **3.** What might the graph look like if both people ate a small snack every 30 minutes instead of a meal?

    a. The levels of both lines would drop faster, as insulin would be used up at a greater rate.

    b. Both lines would spike later, because it would take longer for the blood sugar to accumulate.

    c. Both lines would show more gradual rises at each snack time.

    d. none of the above

Practice

SCIENCE SAMPLE

Directions: Use the bar graph and information provided to answer the questions.

Noise Level of Common Sounds

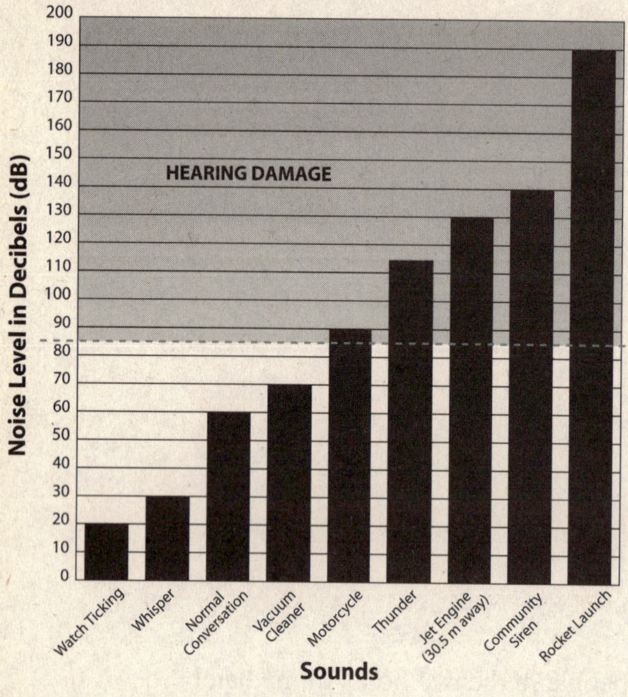

Sources: *The World Book Encyclopedia of Science;* http://www.fda.gov; http://www.sefsc/noaa.gov

Sustained exposure to noise levels above 85 decibels can cause hearing damage.

_____ **1.** Which sound shown on the graph could cause damage to your hearing?
   a. motorcycle
   b. community siren
   c. rocket launch
   d. all of the above

_____ **2.** Which of the following jobs might call for special equipment to protect one's hearing?
   a. radio broadcaster
   b. police officer who directs traffic
   c. airline baggage handler
   d. concert pianist

_____ **3.** The music at a rock concert typically is between 80 and 100 decibels. Where on the graph would a bar representing a rock concert likely fall?
   a. between a motorcycle and thunder
   b. between a watch ticking and a whisper
   c. between a community siren and a rocket launch
   d. between normal conversation and a vacuum cleaner

Answers

THINKING THROUGH THE ANSWERS

Questions from Page 27:

1. **d** is correct. Line B has a larger amount of sugar in the blood for a longer period of time, indicating that there is a lack of insulin to complete the removal process.

   a and **b** are incorrect. The graph gives information about blood sugar levels, not directly about insulin levels.

   c is incorrect. A lower level of sugar indicates that insulin is removing sugar at a normal rate.

2. **b** is correct. The insulin would help remove excess blood sugar, bringing the levels to within the same range as an average person.

   a is incorrect. Line A represents the average person, so it would not change.

   c and **d** are incorrect. These choices cannot be supported by the information given.

3. **c** is correct. The consumption of food will tend to increase blood sugar, but not so much as after eating a full meal. This will create a series of smaller rises.

   a and **b** are incorrect. These choices cannot be supported by the information given.

   d is incorrect. To select this choice, you would need to be able to eliminate each of the other answers.

Questions from Page 28:

1. **d** is correct. All of these sources produce noise above 85 decibels.

   a, b, and **c** are incorrect. Each does not provide a complete answer.

2. **c** is correct. Airline baggage handlers are likely to be exposed to sounds from jet airplanes that could cause hearing damage.

   a, b, and **d** are incorrect. These jobs do not routinely involve sustained exposure to sounds that are damaging.

3. **a** is correct. The range of sound at a rock concert is typically 80–100 dB. Motorcycles are 90 dB and thunder is 115 dB, making this the best answer among the choices given.

   b, c, and **d** are incorrect. The question asks you to consider the most appropriate placement for this range of sound. These choices give ranges significantly higher or significantly lower than that of a rock concert.

Strategies

DIAGRAMS

Diagrams are drawings or sketches that can show structures or concepts. Diagrams may be flowcharts, concept trees, or detailed illustrations with or without labels. Science textbooks use diagrams to present information visually.

❶ Read the title and identify the subject of the diagram.

❷ Read the labels on the diagram. They provide details about the parts shown on the diagram.

❸ Try to draw conclusions from the diagram.

❹ Read the questions, and then study the diagram again.

SCIENCE SAMPLE

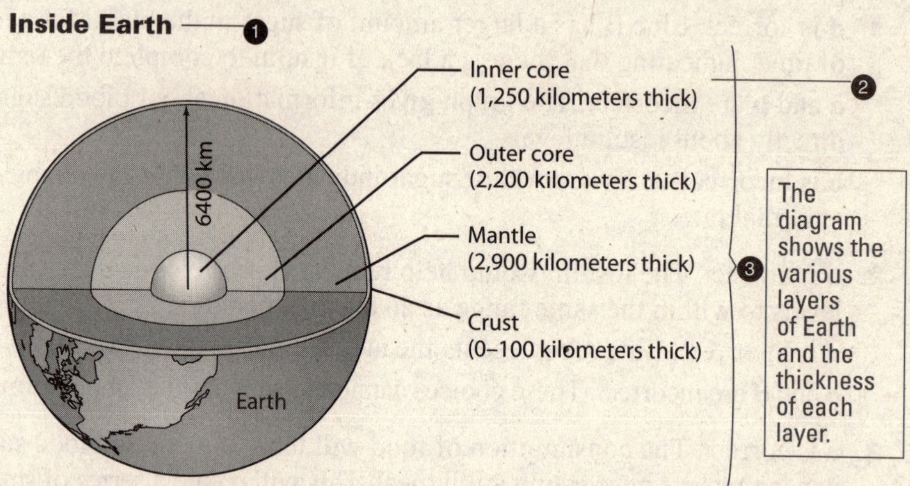

Source: http://pubs.usgs.gov

_____ **1.** Which is the thickest layer of Earth?
   a. outer core
   b. crust
   c. mantle
   d. inner core

_____ **2.** What is the combined thickness of the inner and outer cores?
   a. 1,300 kilometers
   b. 3,450 kilometers
   c. 2,900 kilometers
   d. 100 kilometers

_____ **3.** How thick is the mantle?
   a. 0–100 kilometers
   b. 1,250 kilometers
   c. 2,200 kilometers
   d. 2,900 kilometers

answers: 1. c, 2. b, 3. d

Practice

SCIENCE SAMPLE

Directions: Use the diagram provided to answer the questions.

The Life of Stars

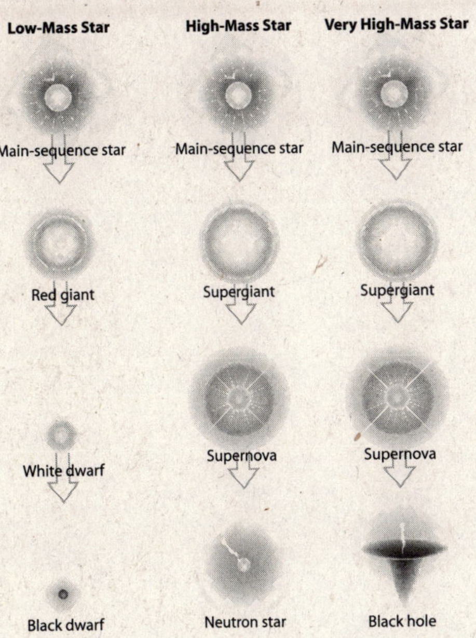

_____ **1.** Which is a possible sequence of the life of a star?

    a. white dwarf ⟶ supernova ⟶ main-sequence star ⟶ supergiant

    b. main-sequence star ⟶ supergiant ⟶ supernova ⟶ neutron star

    c. white dwarf ⟶ neutron star ⟶ black hole

    d. main-sequence star ⟶ white dwarf ⟶ neutron star

_____ **2.** The stage following a supernova explosion may be a black hole or a neutron star. What factor determines which will occur?

    a. whether the star has a high mass or an extremely high mass

    b. how long the main-sequence star stage lasts

    c. how much longer fusion can continue

    d. whether the star has enough helium gas left to create an explosion

_____ **3.** What conclusion can you draw from this diagram?

    a. Most stars are invisible.

    b. Stars change over time.

    c. Stars are all the same size.

    d. All stars become black holes.

Practice

SCIENCE SAMPLE

Directions: Use the diagram to answer the questions.

The Human Skeletal System

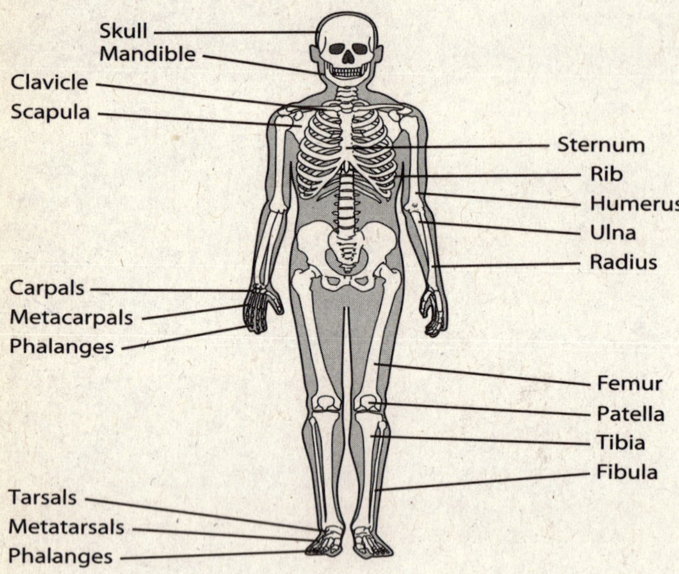

_____ **1.** Which skeletal structures are likely to be involved in grasping a pencil?
   a. sternum and vertebra
   b. femur and patella
   c. metacarpals and phalanges
   d. tarsals and metatarsals

_____ **2.** What is a common name for the mandible?
   a. shoulder
   b. hip
   c. knee
   d. jaw

_____ **3.** Which structures are found in both hands and feet?
   a. phalanges
   b. tarsals
   c. sternum
   d. tibia

Answers

THINKING THROUGH THE ANSWERS

Questions from Page 31:

1. **b** is correct. The diagram shows that a progression from main-sequence star to supergiant to supernova to neutron star is possible.

   a, c, and **d** are incorrect. These choices present sequences that are out of order or not possible.

2. **a** is correct. The diagram shows that the stage after a supernova is determined by the star's mass.

   b is incorrect. There is no evidence to support a conclusion that the length of the main-sequence star stage affects what happens after a supernova.

   c is incorrect. The explosion occurs when fusion can no longer occur. The length of time that fusion continues does not affect the stage following a supernova explosion.

   d is incorrect. The diagram does not support a conclusion concerning the chemical makeup of the star.

3. **b** is correct. The diagram shows the life of stars, which is a series of events. In this case, the events show how stars change over time.

   a is incorrect. Stars are visible in the night sky.

   c is incorrect. Nothing in this diagram indicates that stars are all the same size.

   d is incorrect. The diagram shows that a star can become a white dwarf, a neutron, or a black hole at the end of its life cycle.

Questions from Page 32:

1. **c** is correct. The metacarpals and phalanges are bones in the hand.

   a, b, and **d** are incorrect. The question asks about an activity that one does with the hand. These bones are not related to the hand.

2. **d** is correct. The mandible is the lower jaw.

   a, b, and **c** are incorrect. The label for *mandible* points at the head area. You can eliminate the choices *shoulder, hip,* and *knee* because they do not make sense.

3. **a** is correct. The fingers of the hand and the toes of the feet are composed of bones called phalanges.

   b is incorrect. Tarsals are located only in the feet.

   c and **d** are incorrect. The sternum and the tibia are in neither the hands nor the feet.

Strategies

MAPS

Maps show land features, such as mountains, oceans, and rivers. Thematic maps focus on special topics. For example, a thematic map might show a country's natural resources or land uses.

❶ Read the title of the map. This will give you the subject and purpose of the map.

❷ Read the labels on the map. They also tell about the map's subject and purpose.

❸ Study the key or legend to help you understand the symbols in the map.

❹ Use the scale, if there is one, to estimate distances between places on the map. Map scales usually show the distance in both miles and kilometers.

❺ Read the questions. Carefully study the map to find the answers.

❻ Ask yourself whether the symbols show a pattern.

SCIENCE SAMPLE

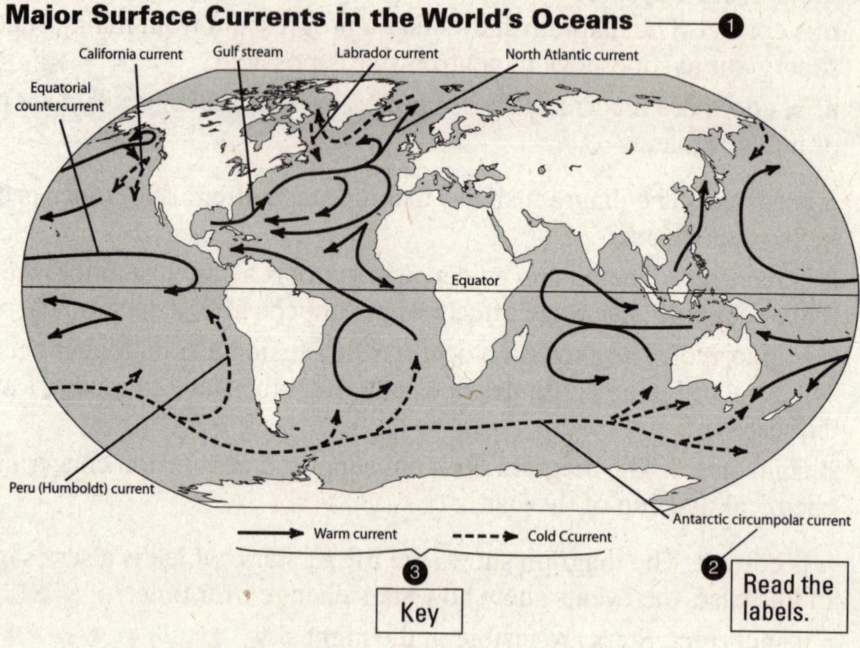

Major Surface Currents in the World's Oceans ❶

Source: http://drifters.doe.gov

_____ **1.** Which hemisphere has more ❺ cool currents?
   a. Eastern Hemisphere
   b. Western Hemisphere
   c. Northern Hemisphere
   d. Southern Hemisphere

_____ **2.** What kind of current is the Equatorial Countercurrent?
   a. warm
   b. cool
   c. polar
   d. inverted

_____ **3.** Which current is likely to have the greatest effect on weather and ocean conditions in the eastern United States?
   a. North Atlantic Current
   b. Gulf Stream
   c. Peru Current
   d. California Current

answers: 1. d, 2. a, 3. b

Practice

SCIENCE SAMPLE

Directions: Use the map to answer the questions.

Human Population Density

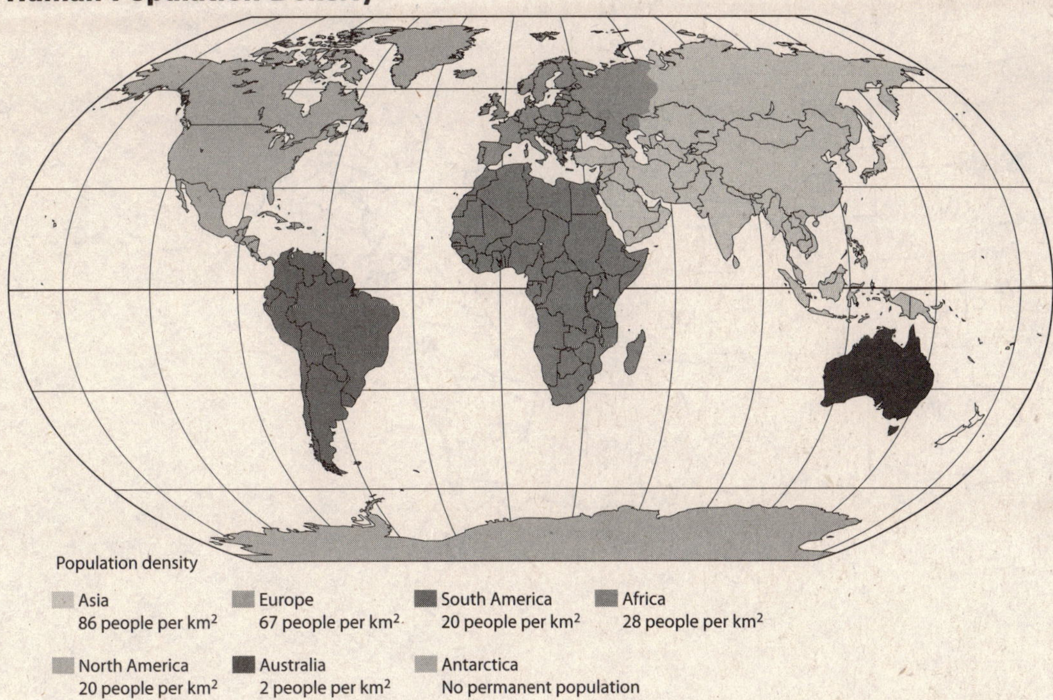

Source: *The World Book Encyclopedia,* 2003

_____ **1.** Which continent, excluding Antarctica, has the lowest population density?

   a. Africa

   b. Asia

   c. Australia

   d. Europe

_____ **2.** Which continent has more than four times the population per square kilometer as South America?

   a. Africa

   b. Asia

   c. Australia

   d. North America

_____ **3.** Antarctica's population density is not represented on the map, because

   a. its population changes dramatically.

   b. it has nearly zero population density.

   c. Antarctica is included as part of North America.

   d. there were too many conflicting population counts.

Practice

SCIENCE SAMPLE

Directions: Use the map and information provided to answer the questions.

Earthquake Hazards in the Continental United States

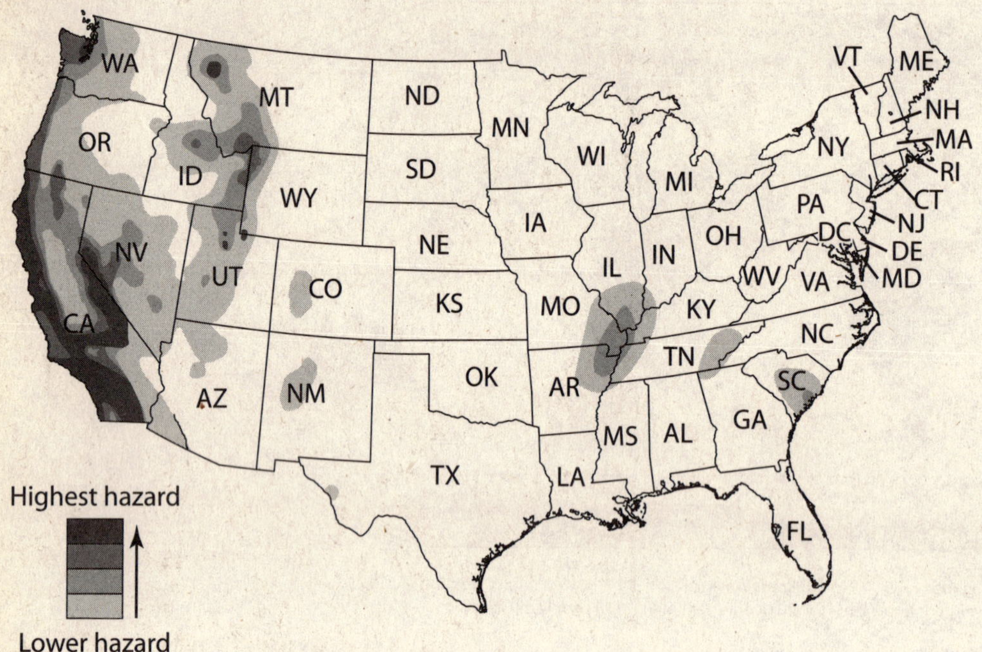

_____ **1.** In which of these states is a major earthquake most likely to occur?

    a. Texas

    b. North Dakota

    c. Colorado

    d. Nevada

_____ **2.** In which of these states is an earthquake least likely to occur?

    a. Colorado

    b. South Carolina

    c. Illinois

    d. Florida

_____ **3.** What conclusion can be drawn from this map?

    a. Homes built in Florida should be constructed to withstand major earthquakes.

    b. Residents of California should keep emergency supplies such as flashlights, food, water, and medicine in the event that an earthquake disrupts services.

    c. Landslides caused by earthquakes are a serious risk to people living in Kansas.

    d. People living in Wisconsin should be prepared to evacuate in the event of a tsunami.

Answers

THINKING THROUGH THE ANSWERS

Questions from Page 35:

1. **c** is correct. Australia has the smallest population, with an average population density of only 2 people per square kilometer.

   a, b, and **d** are incorrect. Africa, Asia, and Europe all have population densities of more than 2 people per square kilometer.

2. **b** is correct. Asia has a population density of 86 people per square kilometer, which is more than four times South America's population density of 19 people per square kilometer.

   a, c, and **d** are incorrect. Africa has less than twice the population density of South America, Australia has a lower population density, and North America has the same population density.

3. **b** is correct. Antarctica's few inhabitants are scientists and researchers who do not reside there permanently.

   a, c, and **d** are incorrect.

Questions from Page 36:

1. **d** is correct. Much of Nevada is at risk for a major earthquake.

   a and **b** are incorrect. The map shows little or no earthquake hazard in Texas and North Dakota.

   c is incorrect. While the map does show some hazard in Colorado, the question asks which is the most likely state. Nevada has a far greater hazard than Colorado.

2. **d** is correct. The map shows that Florida has no earthquake hazards at present.

   a, b, and **c** are incorrect. Colorado, South Carolina, and Illinois all have areas of at least minor earthquake hazard.

3. **b** is correct. Residents of California should take precautions to help them be prepared in the event of an earthquake because the likelihood of a major quake is very high there. This is an appropriate conclusion based on the data shown on the map.

   a, c, and **d** are incorrect. Residents of Florida, Kansas, and Wisconsin have little reason to plan for or fear earthquakes because the likelihood of earthquakes occurring in those states is very small.

Strategies

EXPERIMENTAL DESIGN

Experimental-design questions focus on developing scientific investigations to form and test a hypothesis. The test may ask you to develop your own experimental design based on given information, or it may ask you to identify elements of a given design. Investigations use scientific methods to gather and analyze data. Commonly used scientific methods include determining the problem, making a hypothesis, testing the hypothesis, collecting data, analyzing the results, and drawing conclusions.

1 Read the given information or experimental design to get an idea of the subject.

2 Determine the type of information given. Does the information provide an experimental design or require you to develop your own design?

3 Carefully read the questions. What is the format of the question? Are you asked to choose an answer from given responses or to write your own response?

4 Look for words that help you identify the scientific processes being asked about.

5 If the question requires you to write an extended answer, jot down ideas and use your notes to respond.

SCIENCE SAMPLE

1 You are conducting an experiment in which you observe the rate at which different objects fall. To begin, you have a friend drop a golf **2** ball and a flat sheet of paper from a height of 3 meters. You watch and record which one lands first. Then you take an identical sheet of paper and crumple it to the size and shape of the golf ball. Your friend drops the crumpled paper and the flat sheet of paper from a height of 3 meters. Again you watch and record the results. Finally, your friend drops the golf ball and the crumpled paper from the same height while you watch and record the results.

1. Write a *hypothesis* for the experiment. A hypothesis is a possible **4** explanation for an event. It is a statement or question that identifies what you are testing for.

Possible answer: When the falling objects are about equal in size and shape, they will fall at equal rates. When the falling objects are of different shapes, air resistance will act on the objects in different ways to change the rate of fall.

2. Galileo hypothesized that objects with different masses fall at the same rate. Do you think this experiment is a good way to test his hypothesis? Why or why not?

Possible answer: Yes, the third drop, where the paper is crumpled to the same size and shape as the golf ball, should be a good test for his hypothesis because the objects have different masses.

Practice

SCIENCE SAMPLE

Directions: You want to see how your heart rate changes by doing different activities.
Answer the questions to help plan your experiment.

1. Write a prediction about the way heart rate would be affected by different types of activity.

____

____

____

2. A baseline is a measure that serves as a starting point. A baseline heart rate would be
a heart rate taken while a person is at rest. Explain why finding a baseline heart rate
first is a good idea.

____

____

____

_____ **3.** Which experiment will likely give the most reliable and relevant data?

    a. Have five different people participate in an aerobic activity, measure their
heart rates after 15 minutes, and compare the data.

    b. Select five activities. Check your heart rate after performing each activity.
Compare the data.

    c. Conduct a survey to see which activities people consider most helpful for
cardiovascular health.

    d. Go for a long jog and stop every five minutes to record your heart rate and
see how quickly it rises.

_____ **4.** Which set of five activities would provide the broadest range of data in your
experiment?

    a. reading a book, playing video games, talking on the phone, sleeping,
watching television

    b. jogging, playing tennis, swimming, playing soccer, lifting weights

    c. taking a nap, watching television, walking at a moderate pace, playing
football, running a race

    d. riding a bicycle, shooting baskets, walking at a quick pace, playing catch,
swimming

Practice

SCIENCE SAMPLE

Directions: Use the information provided to answer the questions.

You use the following procedure to model the effect of running water on soil. Take a flat, rectangular pan and fill the bottom with soft clay to represent soil. Place the pan with clay on a table and prop one end of the pan up slightly with a book or two. Using a fountain-like device, attach a tube from the water source onto the elevated end of the pan so that water pours down the pan. At the lower end of the pan, place another tube so that it drains the water out of the pan back into the water source. Observe as the running water erodes the clay.

1. How do you think the water contained in the fountain's water source will change?

2. Explain what the materials you use in your experiment represent.

3. If the water flowed only down the middle of the pan and represented a river, how would the river change over time?

Answers

THINKING THROUGH THE ANSWERS

Questions from Page 39:

1. Use your personal experiences and what you know about heart rates and aerobic activity to make a reasonable prediction about the outcome of the experiment. A reasonable prediction would be that more vigorous activities, such as running, will raise the heart rate most.

2. Since a baseline is a starting point, the heart rate at rest is a good baseline, and it will serve as a control in the experiment. Without a baseline, it wouldn't be possible to note how much an activity actually changes the heart rate.

3. **b** is correct. Having a single subject doing different activities controls for such variables as baseline heart rate while providing data on the effect of several activities.

   a is incorrect. Different people will have different baseline heart rates, and different activities will cause different levels of change.

   c is incorrect. A survey of opinions is not a valid way to test a scientific hypothesis.

   d is incorrect. This experiment tests how heart rate changes with duration of a single activity, not with different activities.

4. **c** is correct. Taking a nap, watching television, walking at a moderate pace, playing football, and running will provide data from both the low end and high end of a range of possible heart rates.

   a, b, and **d** are incorrect. Each of these sets of activities would yield heart rates that are close, so the range of data would not be broad.

Questions from Page 40:

1. The water will get dirty.

2. The clay in the pan is the soil on the hillside. The water at the elevated end is a stream or runoff from a rain. The tube drains the water back to the source.

3. The river will start out straight and fast-moving in a valley with steep sides. Over time, the river will begin to move more slowly, the valley walls will have eroded to become the banks of the river, and the course of the river will have become meandering.

Strategies

EXTENDED RESPONSE

Extended-response questions, like constructed-response questions, usually focus on one kind of exhibit. However, extended-response questions are more complex and require more time to complete than typical constructed-response questions. Some extended-response questions ask you to complete a chart, graph, or diagram. Still others ask you to write an essay or some other, lengthier piece based on the document.

❶ Read the title of the document to get an idea of the subject.

❷ Study and analyze the document. Take notes on your ideas.

❸ Carefully read the extended-response questions.

❹ If the question calls for some type of diagram, make a rough sketch on scrap paper first. Then, make a final copy of your diagram on the answer sheet.

❺ If the question requires a long written response, jot down ideas in outline form. Use this outline to write your answer.

SCIENCE SAMPLE

Escape Velocity —❶

Escape velocity is the velocity a spacecraft or other object must achieve in order to break out of the gravitational pull of a body in space. A more massive body has a stronger gravitational pull and therefore a higher escape velocity. The chart shows the escape velocities from Earth and from several other objects in space.

Object	Escape Velocity (km/sec)
Earth	11.2
Moon	2.4
Sun	618.0
Venus	10.4
Mars	5.0
Jupiter	59.5

Source: http://nssdc.gsfc.gov

❷ The chart shows escape velocities. Not all planets in the solar system are included.

You will need to use information from the paragraph as well as from the chart to make an inference about the data.

1. ❸ Determine how many times greater or less the escape velocities of the other objects are compared to that of Earth. What can you infer about their relative masses based on their escape velocities?

The escape velocity of Earth is about 5 times greater than that of the moon, about 60 times less than that of the Sun, about the same as that of Venus, about twice as much as that of Mars, and about 6 times less than that of Jupiter. Because escape velocity is related to gravitational pull and gravitational pull is related to mass, I can infer that the Sun is the most massive object, followed by Jupiter, Earth, Venus, Mars, and the Moon.

2. Suppose that this relationship between mass and escape velocity were represented on a line graph, with escape velocity represented on the vertical axis and mass represented on the horizontal axis. Sketch a graph that shows the pattern you would expect to see.

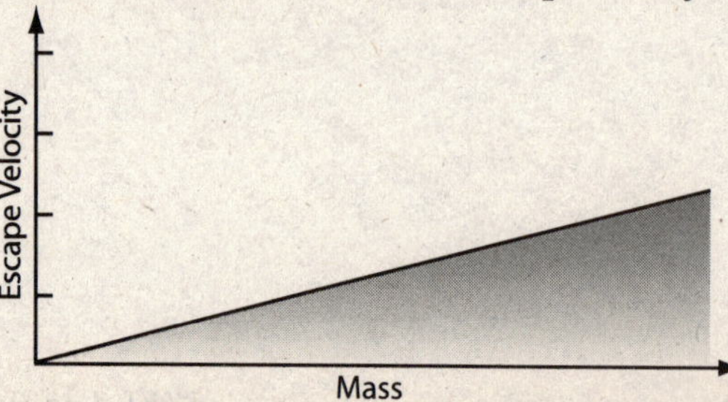

Practice

SCIENCE SAMPLE

Directions: Use the diagram and your knowledge of earth science to answer the following questions.

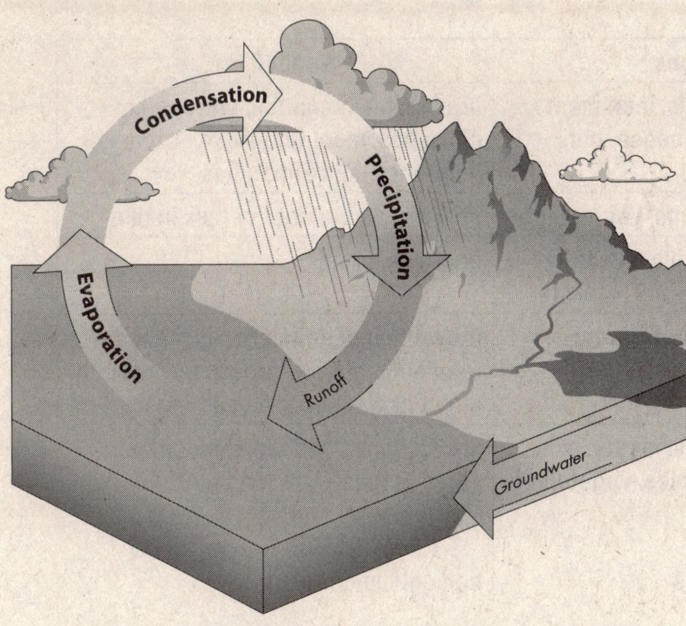

1. Describe three processes in the water cycle.

____

____

____

____

____

____

____

2. Explain how the water cycle continually replenishes Earth's supply of fresh water.

____

____

____

____

____

____

____

Practice

SCIENCE SAMPLE

Directions: Use the table and what you know about life science to answer the questions.

The Six Basic Nutrients

Nutrient	Sources	Needed for
Proteins	soybeans, milk, eggs, lean meats, fish, beans, peas, cheese, nuts	growth, maintenance, and repair of tissues; manufacture of enzymes, hormones, and antibodies
Carbohydrates	cereals, breads, fruits, vegetables	energy source; fiber or bulk in diet
Fats	nuts, butter, vegetable oils, fatty meats, cheese	energy source
Vitamins	milk, butter, lean meats, leafy vegetables, fruits	prevention of deficiency diseases; regulation of body processes; growth; efficient biochemical reactions
Mineral salts (calcium and phosphorus compounds)	whole-grain cereals, meats, milk, green leafy vegetables, vegetables, table salt	strong bones and teeth; blood and other tissues
Iron compounds	meats, nuts, cereals	hemoglobin formation
Iodine	iodized salt, seafoods	production of important hormones in the thyroid gland
Water	all foods	dissolving substances; blood; tissue fluid; biochemical reactions

1. What nutrients are contained in vegetables?

____

____

____

____

2. Consider foods that you enjoy or that are easily available to you. Use the table to plan three meals that include all of these nutrients. Do not repeat any foods.

____

____

____

____

Answers

THINKING THROUGH THE ANSWERS

Questions from Page 43:

1. With evaporation, heat energy from the sun causes water on the earth's surface to change to vapor. The warm vapor rises in the earth's atmosphere, where it cools and condenses into water droplets that form clouds. When the water droplets that form clouds become too many and too heavy to remain afloat in the air, the water falls to earth as precipitation—rain, snow, or hail.

2. **Essay Rubric** The best essays will explain that when water evaporates from the oceans, the salt is left behind. The water vapor condenses into clouds, the clouds move inland, and the water then falls as precipitation into lakes, rivers, ponds, and other fresh water supplies. The water that does not supply lakes, rivers, and ponds or does not become groundwater turns into runoff, which eventually returns to the ocean.

Questions from Page 44:

1. Vegetables contain important nutrients including carbohydrates, vitamins, mineral salts (calcium and phosphorus compounds), and water.

2. Meal plans will vary, but they must include foods that provide all nutrients. The second column, which lists major sources of these nutrients, can be used to generate a list of specific foods. Note that some foods are a source of more than one type of nutrient. For example, milk is a source of proteins, vitamins, mineral compounds, and water.

Strategies

SCENARIO-BASED QUESTIONS

Scenario-based questions are based on information given in a short passage. The passage presents a science-related situation. You use the information to answer multiple-choice or constructed-response questions.

❶ Study and analyze the scenario to get an idea of the subject.

❷ Carefully read the questions. Pay attention to key words in the questions.

❸ Identify the format of the question.

❹ Use the strategies you have learned for the format to help you answer the question.

SCIENCE SAMPLE

Suppose you wanted to measure the volume of an irregularly shaped object, such as a small piece of jagged quartz. The tools you have in front of you are a 1-liter graduated cylinder, a flat-bottomed bowl that the graduated cylinder can be placed in, and a sink. (Remember: 1 milliliter = 1 cubic centimeter.)

❶ The subject of this scenario is measurement.

1. Explain how you could find the volume of the quartz in cubic centimeters using the objects available to you.

❸ This question is a constructed-response question.

Place the graduated cylinder in the bowl and fill the cylinder completely with water. Place the piece of quartz into the graduated cylinder. Measure the amount of water that overflows from the cylinder. The amount of water (in milliliters) will equal the volume of the quartz piece in centimeters cubed.

2. What does this type of measuring depend upon?

❸ This question is a multiple-choice question.

   a. oxidation—the process of oxygen being added to an element or compound

   b. graduation—the series of marks on a container representing quantity

   c. displacement—placing an object in a liquid that causes the volume in a container to increase

   d. hydrolysis—the decomposition of a compound due to reaction with water

answers: 1. See above, 2. c

Practice

SCIENCE SAMPLE

Directions: Read the scenario and use the information it provides to answer the questions.

Kelly sets up two inclines. She lines one with foil and one with sandpaper. Then she places equally sized and shaped blocks of smooth wood at the top of each incline. She lets go of the blocks and lets them slide down the inclines. The one on the foil slides easily. The one on the sandpaper does not.

_____ **1.** What concept is illustrated by Kelly's activity?

   a. the causes of inertia

   b. the chemical reactions between wood and various materials

   c. the effects of friction on moving objects

   d. the probability of acceleration

_____ **2.** If Kelly replaced the wood blocks with metal coins, how would the outcome be different?

   a. The coins would probably stick to both surfaces.

   b. The coins would probably go down both inclines faster.

   c. The coin on the foil-covered incline would not move very easily.

   d. none of the above

_____ **3.** If Kelley replaced each of the blocks with a heavier block and repeated the experiment, what would you predict the results would be?

   a. The block in the sandpaper pan would move slower.

   b. The block in the foil pan would move slower.

   c. Both blocks would move faster.

   d. Both blocks would move slower.

Practice

SCIENCE SAMPLE

Directions: Read the scenario and use the information it provides to answer the questions.

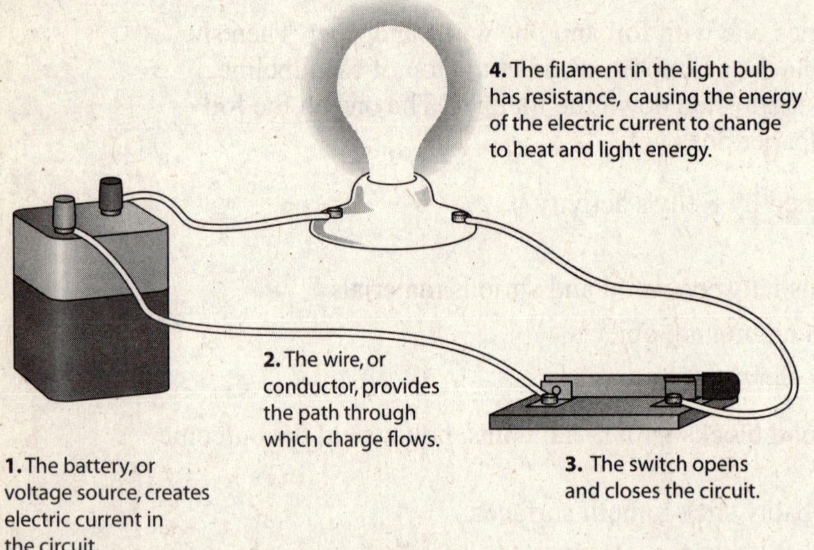

Jacob built a circuit. Using wire, he connected a battery to a switch, the switch to a light socket with a bulb, and the light socket back to the battery. The battery is good, but the light bulb is not coming on, so he knows the circuit isn't closed.

_____ **1.** Which of the following explains why the circuit is not closed?
   a. The switch is not closed.
   b. A wire is not connected properly.
   c. The filament in the bulb is broken.
   d. all of the above

_____ **2.** If Jacob replaces the switch with another light bulb, will both light bulbs light up?
   a. No, only the first will receive enough electricity to light up.
   b. Yes, the switch was keeping the circuit open, so replacing it with a light bulb will close the circuit and light the bulbs.
   c. Yes, the two bulbs will create a closed circuit between themselves, causing the lights to come on.
   d. A result cannot be determined from the information given.

3. In the original setup, is Jacob's circuit a series circuit or a parallel circuit? Explain.

____

____

____

____

____

Answers

THINKING THROUGH THE ANSWERS

Questions from Page 47:

1. **c** is correct. The sandpaper creates a high-friction surface, and the foil creates a low-friction surface, so the activity is a good way to see how friction slows down different objects.

   a is incorrect. Inertia is the tendency for objects to stay in whatever state of motion they are in. The inclines introduce the force of gravity, which is acting to overcome inertia. The activity does nothing to illustrate inertia.

   b is incorrect. No chemical reactions are taking place in the movement of the blocks.

   d is incorrect. There is no indication that acceleration is being considered in the activity.

2. **b** is correct. The smooth surface of the metal would be less likely to experience friction against either the foil or the sandpaper, so the coins will likely move faster than the wood blocks.

   a and **c** are incorrect. It is unlikely that the smoother surface of the coins would experience much friction on either surface.

   d is incorrect. *None of the above* is a valid choice only when you can reasonably eliminate all other choices.

3. **c** is correct. The heavier the blocks, the faster they would move down the incline. **a, b,** and **d** are incorrect, as the blocks would not move slower.

Questions from Page 48:

1. **d** is correct. Each of the choices describes a factor that would keep the circuit open, therefore keeping the light bulb from lighting.

   a, b, and **c** are correct. When more than one choice is correct, look for an answer that includes multiple choices, such as *all of the above.*

2. **d** is correct. The light bulbs would both light only if the switch was what was keeping the circuit open. Without knowing what was keeping the circuit open in the first place, it is not possible to say whether the light bulbs will light.

   a is incorrect. Provided that the circuit is closed, both light bulbs would light.

   b is incorrect. This would be true only if the switch was what was keeping the circuit open in the first place. However, the scenario does not say why the circuit could not close.

   c is incorrect. Two bulbs without an electricity source cannot create a closed circuit between themselves.

3. Jacob's circuit is a series circuit because the setup provides a single path for the electrons to take. A parallel circuit would provide more than one path.

Test Practice

The questions that follow illustrate the types of items found on many tests or formal assessments. Use these questions as models for preparing for tests. After you have taken the test, check the answers on page 64. If you find you consistently miss one type of question, return to the strategies pages in Part 2. Review the strategies for answering the type of questions you missed.

_____ **1.** According to the system of binomial nomenclature, which is always the first word in a scientific name?

    a. kingdom

    b. genus

    c. class

    d. species

2. Define the science of taxonomy.

____

____

____

_____ **3.** Where is Earth's magnetic field strongest?

    a. around the equator

    b. around the prime meridian

    c. around the North Pole and South Pole

    d. all of the above

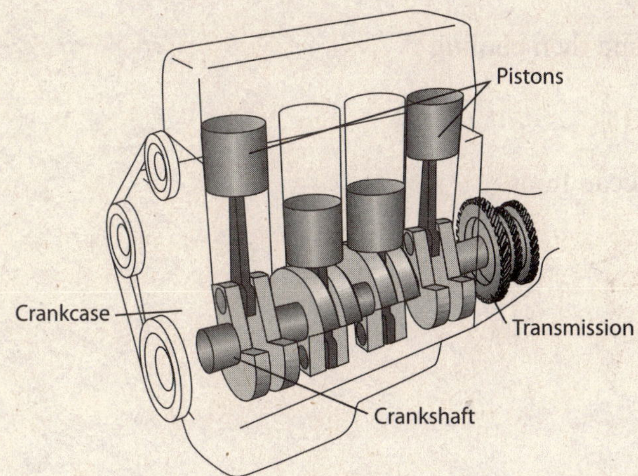

_____ **4.** Which simple machine is part of the engine shown in the diagram?

    a. wheel and axle

    b. inclined plane

    c. wedge

    d. pulley

_____ **5.** Heat transfers from warmer objects to cooler objects in three ways. Which is NOT a form of heat transfer?

    a. convection

    b. conduction

    c. condensation

    d. radiation

_____ **6.** What is contained in the nucleus of an atom?

    a. protons and neutrons

    b. electrons and isotopes

    c. energy levels and electron clouds

    d. all of the above

_____ **7.** Which of these living things is in the kingdom Monera?

    a. shrimp

    b. celery

    c. bacteria

    d. mushrooms

_____ **8.** What two factors influence climate?

    a. temperature and precipitation

    b. rain and snow

    c. wind and humidity

    d. ocean currents and time of year

_____ **9.** Which process is part of soil formation?

    a. magma rising through Earth's crust and then cooling

    b. lakes and rivers drying out

    c. rocks broken down by weathering

    d. decayed marine life settling on the ocean floor

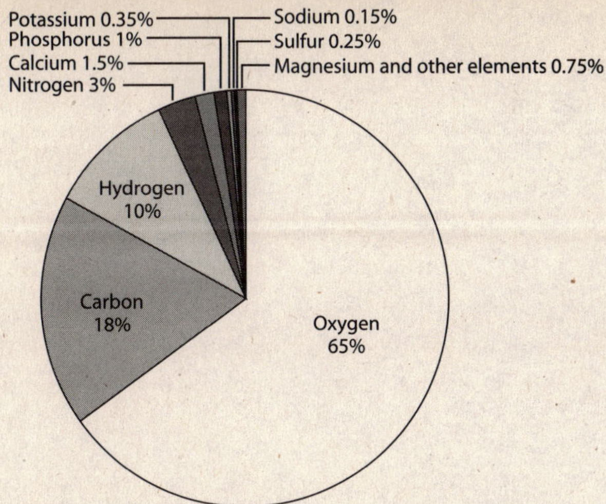

Source: http://chemistry.about.com/cs/howthingswork

_____ **10.** How much of your body is composed of nonmetals?

    a. a tiny percent

    b. one-third

    c. exactly half

    d. more than two-thirds

11. Most of these elements make up compounds in your body. What compound do you think most of your body's hydrogen and oxygen make up?

____

_____ **12.** What information is contained in an element's square on the periodic table?

    a. atomic symbol

    b. atomic number

    c. atomic mass

    d. all of the above

_____ **13.** Which is a characteristic of protozoa?

    a. They are unicellular.

    b. They cannot make their own food.

    c. They are larger than bacteria.

    d. all of the above

_____ **14.** Which is true of a virus?

    a. It is made up of many cells.

    b. It is made up of only one cell.

    c. It is not made up of cells at all.

    d. It is classified in the bacteria kingdom.

_____ **15.** How were many freshwater resources, such as the Great Lakes, formed?

    a. by flooding from the ocean

    b. from oxbow lakes of rivers

    c. from precipitation

    d. by glaciers

_____ **16.** From left to right across a period on the periodic table, what happens to atomic size?

    a. It increases.

    b. It decreases.

    c. It randomly increases and decreases.

    d. It remains the same.

Electricity Used by Appliances Operated for Two Hours Daily for One Year

Appliance	Kilowatt Hours per Year
Microwave oven	730
Clothes washer	329
Clothes dryer	2,920
Dishwasher	1,460
Vacuum cleaner	876
Personal computer	270
27-inch television	82

Source: http://www.eere.energy.gov

_____ **17.** If you use each of these appliances two hours every day for a year, which appliance would cost you the most on your electricity bill?

    a. personal computer

    b. clothes washer

    c. clothes dryer

    d. dishwasher

18. Would you use more electricity watching television for an hour or running a dishwasher for an hour? Explain the reason for your answer.

____

____

____

_____ **19.** How are algae different from plants?

    a. Algae contain chlorophyll.

    b. Algae do not produce flowers or seeds.

    c. Algae make their own food.

    d. all of the above

_____ **20.** Which kingdom includes single-celled organisms?

    a. Animalia

    b. Plantae

    c. Protista

    d. Fungi

_____ **21.** What is the most abundant gas in Earth's atmosphere?
    a. oxygen
    b. nitrogen
    c. carbon dioxide
    d. hydrogen

_____ **22.** What two organisms make up a lichen?
    a. a fungus and an alga
    b. a vascular plant and a nonvascular plant
    c. a bacterium and a protozoan
    d. an animal and a plant

_____ **23.** Which statement is true of ferns?
    a. Ferns are vascular plants.
    b. Ferns belong to the Fungi kingdom.
    c. Ferns have flowers and fruit.
    d. Ferns are extinct.

_____ **24.** What is the ocean zone where the temperature is lowest?
    a. surface zone
    b. thermocline
    c. deep zone
    d. all of the above

_____ **25.** What describes a chemical reaction in which energy is released?
    a. endothermic
    b. exothermic
    c. balanced
    d. none of the above

Testing Radiant Energy

David measured the temperature of a cup of soil and the temperature of a cup of
water that had been sitting in a shaded area for several hours. Then he placed the cup
of soil and the cup of water next to each other under a desk lamp. After ten minutes,
he measured the temperatures of the materials inside the cups again.

_____ **26.** How do you think the temperatures of the two materials would have been related
after the first reading in the shade?
   a. The soil would have been much warmer than the water.
   b. The water would have been much warmer than the soil.
   c. The temperatures would have been about the same.
   d. The soil would have been slightly above freezing and the water slightly below.

_____ **27.** Would the soil or the water have been warmer after sitting under the desk lamp? Why?

____

____

____

_____ **28.** What is another name for a flowering plant?
   a. nonvascular plant
   b. angiosperm
   c. stamen
   d. gymnosperm

_____ **29.** About what percentage of Earth's water is fresh water?
   a. 3 percent
   b. 13 percent
   c. 30 percent
   d. 63 percent

_____ **30.** How are acids different from bases?
   a. Acids react to certain chemicals; bases do not.
   b. Acids are corrosive; bases are not.
   c. Acids conduct electricity; bases do not.
   d. Acids taste sour; bases taste bitter.

Holography

Standard pictures record images in two dimensions, but holographic images add a third dimension. A hologram has the depth and texture of the original object. Holograms are created with lasers. The lasers form light patterns of an object on holographic plates, which are then used to make the hologram itself. Holograms are used on credit cards, in instruments that scan bar codes, and in aviation to train pilots. However, some scientists expect that a day will come when holograms will be a part of almost everything we see around us.

_____ **31.** Which is an advantage of holography over regular photography?

    a. Machines that take holograms are less likely to break than cameras.

    b. Holograms are quicker and cheaper to develop than photographs.

    c. Holograms include a third dimension for a closer representation of the original object.

    d. all of the above

32. Explain one way you think holographic images might be used in the future.

____

____

____

_____ **33.** What are the three main classification groups of worms used by scientists?

    a. flatworms, roundworms, and segmented worms

    b. red worms, green worms, and reticulated worms

    c. fuzzy worms, smooth worms, and slimy worms

    d. long worms, short worms, and thin worms

_____ **34.** Which phylum includes starfish?

    a. mollusks

    b. echinoderms

    c. arthropods

    d. coelenterates

_____ **35.** Why is Earth's iron and nickel core solid despite its 5,000°C temperature?

    a. Pressure from the layers above causes it to remain solid.

    b. The inner core is too massive to be melted.

    c. The melting point of iron and nickel is higher than 5,000°C.

    d. Earthquakes and volcanoes cool the inner core.

_____ **36.** What is acceleration?

    a. distance traveled per unit of time

    b. speed in a given direction

    c. change in velocity per unit of time

    d. velocity of a car

_____ **37.** Which characteristic is NOT shared by all birds?

    a. They lay eggs.

    b. Their front legs are modified into wings.

    c. They are invertebrates.

    d. They are ectothermic.

38. Explain how plate tectonics can cause a mountain range to form.

____

____

____

_____ **39.** What are three types of volcanoes?

    a. active, irregular, and dormant

    b. mountain, hill, and pyramid

    c. elongated, narrow, and pointed

    d. shield, composite, and cinder cone

_____ **40.** What is kinetic energy?

    a. energy of motion

    b. stored energy

    c. gravitational energy

    d. all of the above

The Inner Planets

Name	Average Distance from Sun (million km)	Diameter (km)	Period of Revolution in Earth Time	Period of Rotation	Surface Temperature Extremes (degrees Celsius)
Mercury	58	4,878	88 days	59 days	High 427/Low −180
Venus	108	12,104	225 days	243 days	High 482/Low −482
Earth	150	12,756	365 days	24 hours	High 58/Low −89
Mars	228	6,794	686 days	25 hours	High 0/Low −129

Sources: http://www.windows.ucar.edu; http://nssdc.gsfc.gov

_____ **41.** Why does Mars take the longest to revolve around the Sun?

    a. because it has the largest diameter

    b. because its cold surface temperatures slow it down

    c. because it is farthest from the Sun

    d. all of the above

_____ **42.** Which planet has the largest range in temperature?

    a. Mercury

    b. Venus

    c. Earth

    d. Mars

_____ **43.** Skeletal muscles are classified as

    a. voluntary muscles.

    b. involuntary muscles.

    c. cardiac muscles.

    d. none of the above

_____ **44.** What function do platelets perform?

    a. control bleeding

    b. bring oxygen to the brain

    c. aid in digestion

    d. maintain temperature

_____ **45.** Which law states that a layer of sedimentary rock is older than the one above it?

    a. law of stacking

    b. law of superposition

    c. law of rock history

    d. all of the above

_____ **46.** The wheel and axle, the wedge, the screw, and the lever are four of the six simple machines. What are the other two?

    a. shovel and broom

    b. hammer and compass

    c. rope and chain

    d. pulley and inclined plane

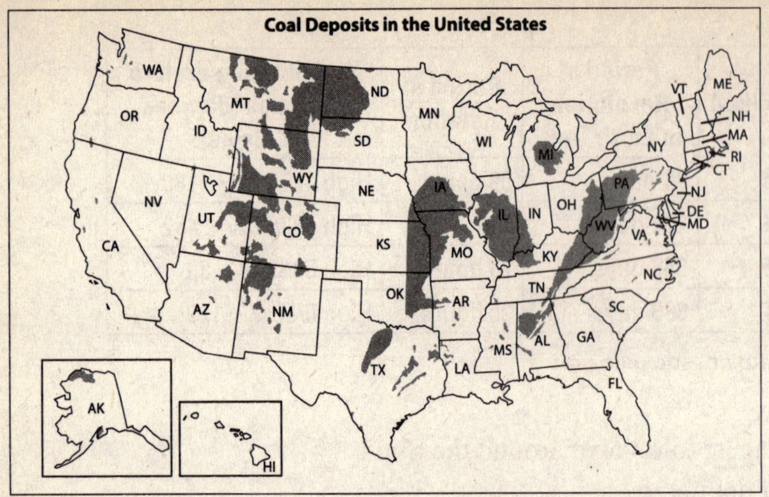

Source: *The World Book Encyclopedia,* 2003

_____ **47.** How are the coal reserves distributed throughout the United States?

    a. They are concentrated primarily on the West Coast.

    b. They form a solid column from Minnesota to Louisiana.

    c. They exist mostly in the southern states.

    d. They are spread around much of the United States.

48. Coal was formed from the remains of plants in ancient swamps. What conclusion can you draw about the Appalachian Mountains in the eastern United States?

____

____

_____ **49.** In the digestive system, starches are broken down into

    a. fatty acids.

    b. amino acids.

    c. simple sugars.

    d. proteins.

_____ **50.** Which system includes the lungs, nostrils, and trachea?

    a. digestive system

    b. respiratory system

    c. nervous system

    d. circulatory system

_____ **51.** All of the following provide evidence for evolution EXCEPT

    a. the fossil record.

    b. the presence of vestigial and homologous organs.

    c. erosion.

    d. embryology.

52. Define specific heat.

____

____

The Human Skeletal System

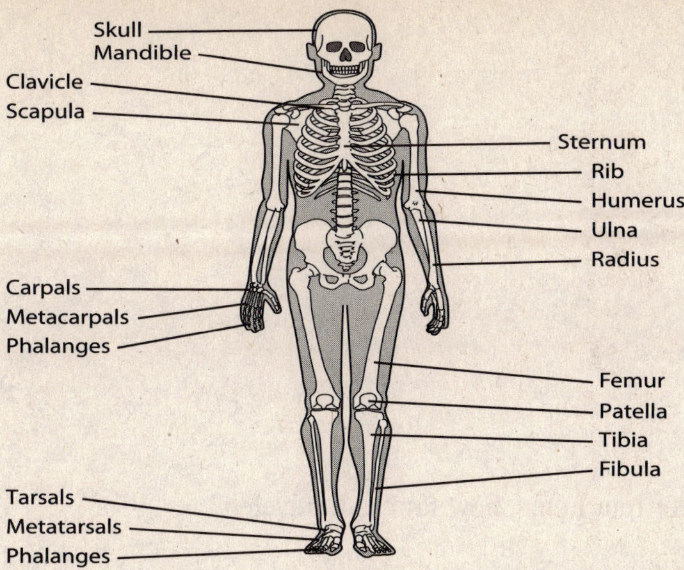

_____ **53.** Which part of the human body contains the most bones?

    a. the jaw

    b. the knee

    c. the shoulder

    d. the hand

54. Describe how joints move in the following activities: Walking, chewing, and turning your head.

____

____

_____ **55.** Where is urine stored?

    a. in the urea

    b. in the kidneys

    c. in the urinary bladder

    d. all of the above

_____ **56.** Which body part belongs to the nervous system?

    a. spinal cord

    b. nerves

    c. brain

    d. all of the above

_____ **57.** What is the process of splitting an atom to release energy called?

    a. nuclear fusion

    b. nuclear fission

    c. atomic reconditioning

    d. atomic relocation

58. Define metamorphosis.

____

____

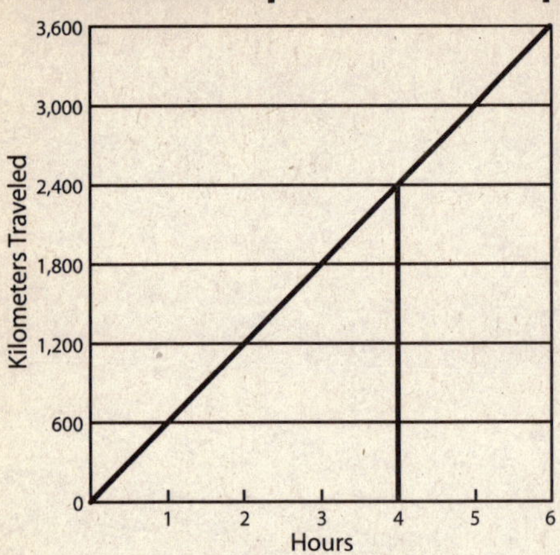

_____ **59.** When the jetliner lands for fuel after four hours, how far has it traveled?

    a. 1,200 kilometers

    b. 1,800 kilometers

    c. 2,400 kilometers

    d. 3,000 kilometers

_____ **60.** How would the graph be different if it showed the time it took to build up speed after takeoff and the time it took to reduce speed before landing?

    a. The graph line would not be straight.

    b. The increments on the vertical and horizontal would be different.

    c. The line graph would have to be changed to a bar graph.

    d. all of the above

_____ **61.** Which system works in conjunction with the nervous system to regulate or control other parts of the body?

    a. circulatory system

    b. digestive system

    c. endocrine system

    d. excretory system

_____ **62.** Which of the following is a renewable resource?

    a. solar energy

    b. water

    c. geothermal energy

    d. all of the above

63. How do human activities affect acid rain?

____

____

_____ **64.** Electricity can flow only through what type of circuit?

    a. an open circuit

    b. a closed circuit

    c. a shorted circuit

    d. all of the above

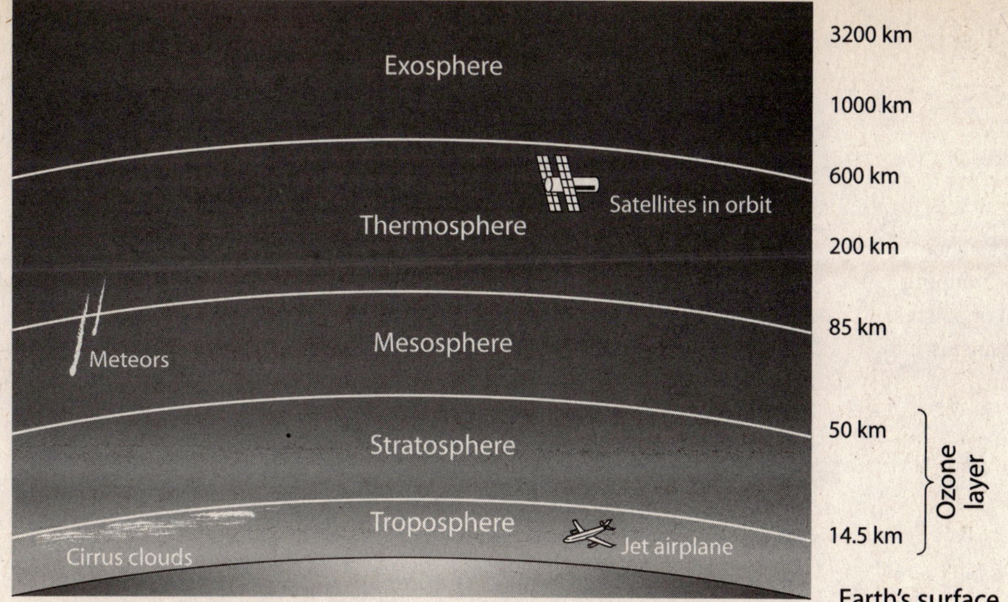

Source: http://liftoff.msfc.nasa.gov

_____ **65.** In which layer of Earth's atmosphere is the ozone layer found?

    a. troposphere

    b. stratosphere

    c. mesosphere

    d. thermosphere

_____ **66.** In which layer of Earth's atmosphere do most meteoroids burn up?

    a. troposphere

    b. stratosphere

    c. mesosphere

    d. thermosphere

Answer Key

Part 3

TEST PRACTICE

1. **b**

2. Taxonomy is the science of classification (grouping and naming) that organizes all of Earth's organisms into an ordered system.

3. **c**

4. **a**

5. **d**

6. **a**

7. **c**

8. **a**

9. **c**

10. **d**

11. Most of the human body is made up of water, so the elements hydrogen and oxygen exist mostly as water.

12. **d**

13. **d**

14. **c**

15. **d**

16. **a**

17. **c**

18. The dishwasher would use more electricity than the television because the dishwasher requires more energy to run.

19. **b**

20. **c**

21. **b**

22. **a**

23. **a**

24. **c**

25. **b**

26. **c**

27. The soil would have been warmer because solids absorb radiant energy faster than liquids.

28. **b**

29. **a**

30. **d**

31. **c**

32. Answers will vary.

33. **a**

34. **b**

35. **a**

36. **c**

37. **c**

38. When two continental plates collide, their edges may crumple and be pushed up, or the edge of one plate may be lifted up and over the edge of the other, creating mountains.

39. **d**

40. **a**

41. **c**

42. **a**

43. **a**

44. **a**

45. **b**

46. **d**

47. **d**

48. The Appalachian Mountains must at one time long ago have been low swamplands.

49. **c**

50. **b**

51. **c**

52. Specific heat is the capacity of a substance to absorb heat energy.

53. **d**

54. Sample Answers: Walking is made possible by joints in the hip as well as joints at the knee. Chewing is made possible by joints at the jaw. Turning your head is made possible by pivot joints.

55. **c**

56. **d**

57. **b**

58. Sample Answer: Metamorphosis is the process in which animals go through changes in body form as they develop.

59. **c**

60. **a**

61. **c**

62. **d**

63. Humans burn coal, gas, and oil from cars, factories, and power plants. The process makes gases that result in acid rain.

64. **b**

65. **b**

66. **c**